RANGER REDEMPTION

BROTHERHOOD PROTECTORS COLORADO BOOK #3

ELLE JAMES

TWISTED PAGE INC

RANGER REDEMPTION

BROTHERHOOD PROTECTORS COLORADO
BOOK #3

New York Times & USA Today
Bestselling Author

ELLE JAMES

Dedicated to Bandit and Charli who keep me on my toes and love me unconditionally. I love my two Yorkies!
Elle James

AUTHOR'S NOTE

Enjoy other military books by Elle James

Visit ellejames.com for titles and release dates
For hot cowboys, visit her alter ego Myla Jackson at
mylajackson.com
and join Elle James's Newsletter at
https://ellejames.com/contact/

CHAPTER 1

"Yeah, well, here we are." Cage Weaver stood at the top of Pikes Peak, breathing hard, his legs shaky from pushing himself hard on the ascent. He shrugged out of the backpack he'd worn all the way to the top, carrying the six pounds of what was left of his battle buddy and best friend, Ryan Meyers.

"You know this wasn't how we were supposed to do this race. You and I were supposed to complete this marathon together, in competition, not me carrying your sorry ass to the top."

His chest squeezed hard. Cage blamed the altitude. At over fourteen thousand feet, anyone would be sucking wind. Especially after the grueling run up the mountain. Thirteen miles of trail and an elevation change of over seventy-eight hundred feet took it out of a person. Even if he was in great shape.

Ryan had dreamed of the ascent. They'd signed up

for the race over a year in advance, planning to complete it together once they returned from deployment to Afghanistan. The only problem was that Ryan came back in a body bag. Cage was forced to fulfill Ryan's dream on his own.

"Well, not quite on my own," Cage said, hefting the box containing the ashes of his friend. "Now, all I have left to do is release your ashes here at the summit, like I promised." He started to open the box.

Before he could release the latch, a crowd of half-marathon competitors arrived at the top, racing past the finish line to loud cheers. Those running the full twenty-six plus miles would be heading back down the mountain. Everywhere Cage turned, someone was standing, taking up space on the peak and snapping photos of each other. He couldn't release Ryan's ashes without someone seeing him do it.

Not only was the release of his friend's final remains a private occasion, but it was also prohibited at the summit of Pikes Peak as per park regulations.

Cage glanced around. With all the people standing around congratulating each other over reaching the summit, he wouldn't find a private place to slip Ryan's ashes out of the box and into the wind.

With time ticking away on his watch and the remainder of the marathon yet to complete, he shoved Ryan's box back into his backpack, zipped it and looked around at the men and women who'd made it to the top thus far.

He might have found a way to release Ryan's ashes had he stayed longer. The truth was, he wasn't ready to let go of his friend. Not on the battlefield and not on Pikes Peak.

He slipped the backpack over his shoulders and joined the others on the race back down the mountain.

At least he'd completed part of his promise to Ryan as he'd held his buddy in his arms while he'd bled out from grievous wounds he'd suffered from a mortar round explosion. He and Ryan would complete the Pikes Peak Marathon together.

He'd fulfill his other promise to spread his buddy's ashes on a mountain in Colorado another day.

It would have to wait until his next chance to summit a mountain. Cage was due to start a new job tomorrow. He'd been assured the work would utilize his skills as a soldier and make his transition to the civilian world less painful.

He'd be the judge of that once he got his feet wet with the Brotherhood Protectors Colorado division.

"How did everybody do with the techniques we discussed last week at our session?" Emily Strayhorn asked the group of ten veterans who sat in a semi-circle for their weekly PTSD therapy.

When nobody raised his hand, she called on each, one by one. "How about you, JR?"

Staff Sergeant Jason Ryan Slater, who preferred to be called JR, shrugged. "I tried, but I'm still having nightmares."

She smiled gently. "That's to be expected after what you went through."

Former Army Ranger JR Slater had been in a fierce firefight against the Taliban. When he'd been hit by shrapnel from a grenade, he'd lost two of his buddies and his left leg. He, like the others in the group, were there dealing with PTSD from battle-related events.

It was Emily's job to help them recover from not their physical wounds, but their mental wounds that would likely plague them for the rest of their lives. She knew she couldn't erase the memories, but she hoped to give them tools and techniques to deal with them.

"Meditation won't cure the nightmares. Hopefully, it will help you learn how to cope with your feelings." She turned to a young man with long hair and dark shadows beneath his eyes. "How about you, Jimmy?"

Jimmy Rhodes had been the victim of an IED explosion that had hit his truck. He'd survived by playing dead when the Taliban overran his position. Trapped beneath the heavy truck, he'd lain for hours until rescued. He had nightmares about that day and couldn't focus his thoughts for more than a couple minutes at a time. "I don't see how meditation can help. I sat like you told me to, closed my eyes, and then I thought of a thousand things I needed to be doing. All of them involved moving, not sitting still."

"Meditation is like physical exercise," Emily said. "The more you flex your muscles, the easier it gets."

"I just don't see the point," Jimmy said.

And there were other nods amongst the veterans.

"The idea is not just to close your eyes but to focus on one thing and one thing only, otherwise your mind becomes like a ball in a pinball machine, with your thoughts bouncing in every direction."

"I tried it, Dr. Strayhorn." Nathan Small raised his hand. "It worked for me. I focused on one thing. It helped me to clear my thoughts of anything else."

Emily turned to Nathan and smiled. "That's good. Were you able to focus for very long?"

He nodded. "I was, and you were right. It gave me some really clear thinking. And that focus remained with me through the night. I didn't have one nightmare."

"That's good, Nathan." She turned to the others. "I understand your hesitation. You are men who have been used to constant motion and adrenaline rushes. Unless you're mountain climbing or sky diving every day of the week, you're probably not going to burn off that energy. You need ways to calm that inner anxiety and the need to move."

Some of the men frowned.

Emily held up a hand. "I'm not saying that meditation is the only way. It should be used in combination with exercise. Remember that exercise can take many forms…running, jogging, weightlifting, hiking, climbing and playing. Don't discount playing. Join some kind of community sports team. There are a lot of them out there. That will help you with the physical release. The meditation will help you with the thoughts bouncing around inside your head like a ping pong ball. During those quiet times, if you aren't exercising or playing, pick something that makes you happy and focus on it to the point you clear your mind of all else. Again, the more you practice, the better you'll be at it."

Several of the veterans glanced at their watches. Emily did, too, and realized they'd gone a couple minutes past their time. None of them had really wanted to be in the therapy sessions, but they'd been urged to go by family members or their former or current commanders, for those who were still on active duty and struggling with PTSD.

"Well, gentlemen, that concludes our session. I urge you to continue to try to do the meditation techniques I've shown you. At least give it a couple of weeks. Even fifteen minutes a day will help. And as always, thank you for your service. You men are the heroes our country needs."

A couple of them snorted as they rose from their chairs and headed for the exit.

One muttered, "Heroes don't have nightmares."

"Or need therapy," another responded.

They were wrong. Heroes were like everyone else. They got scared, had nightmares and suffered after traumatic events. The difference was that they had courage when it was needed.

Emily was the last one out of the room. She switched off the light then closed and locked the door. She hurried down the long hall to her office where she made notes in her electronic medical record about the various patients and their reactions during the group therapy session.

She had been with the veterans' hospital for the past four years, working with veterans with various difficulties, mostly battle-related PTSD and PTSD brought on by military sexual trauma.

After she'd graduated with her doctorate in psychology, she could have gone to work in any civilian office and made more money, but that wasn't where her heart was. She wanted to give back to her country by helping veterans who'd sacrificed so much. She would have joined the military, but she hadn't qualified for active duty because of a physical disability that caused her to walk with a slight limp.

When she'd been seventeen years old, her family had been involved in an automobile accident. While her parents and her younger brother had been killed in the accident, her life had been spared, leaving her with no family and a mangled leg. The orthopedic surgeon had been able to put her leg back together with pins and surgery, but she'd never run marathons and she would never be able to meet the physical requirements of any branch of service.

Not that she had been considering the military as a post high school graduation career, but losing her parents had left her orphaned at seventeen. With one year left in high school and college acceptance letters already coming in, she had been left homeless and without a family

One of her classmates, RJ Tate, had learned of her plight, spoken to her former military father and come up with a solution. Emily had moved in with Dan Tate, or Gunny, as he preferred to be addressed, and his daughter RJ. Having a home in her school district allowed Emily to finish high school with top honors. Her parents would have wanted that.

Emily had powered through her grief, focusing on everything her mother and father had wanted her to achieve. Whenever she'd been down, Gunny and RJ had helped lift her spirits. She'd worked hard at her schoolwork, but she'd also worked hard on the ranch —mucking stalls, mending fences and taking care of animals.

Gunny was a disciplined man. He'd had them up early to do all the chores before they'd gone to school. The man was also fair to a fault, never asking them to do anything he wasn't willing to do himself. He'd had them digging holes for fence posts and staying up late into the night to nurse a sick animal. They'd learned by his example.

His years in the military had taught him how to be tough, although Emily suspected he'd been born that way. The man never slowed down. Even now, he ran a ranch and a bar with the help of his daughter. He had a habit of taking in strays like herself and their friend JoJo, employing them when they needed spending money and giving them a place to stay when they had nowhere else to go.

Emily finished her notes, logged off her computer and left her office, locking it behind her. The VA hospital never closed, but her area of the building was deserted by the time she left. She figured she had just enough time to go home, change into something else and head out to the Lost Valley Ranch.

Gunny and RJ had invited her out for a late supper, with RJ's friend JoJo and some of Gunny's long-term tenants, who'd rented the entire basement of the ranch house for a new division of a Montana-based company started by a veteran and employing veterans. The ones she'd met so far were great guys.

Surprisingly, JoJo and RJ had fallen in love with a couple of them. It made Emily happy to see them happy. Maybe someday, Emily would find that kind of happiness as well with someone who could accept her as she was, limp and all.

Tired from working with people with real emotional and mental problems all day long, she was ready to blow the cobwebs from her head and breathe in some of that cool mountain air.

When she reached her car, she fumbled in her purse for her keys, her hand on the door handle. She tugged on the door handle. As expected, it didn't open, proof that she'd locked it that morning like she did every morning. Finally, she found her key. The sun still shone bright as it slipped toward the peaks. The rays glinted off the window blinding her. She hit the unlock button and heard the snick of the locks disengaging.

When she opened the door and started to throw her purse into the passenger floorboard, she paused. On the driver's seat lay a single red rose.

She stared down at the flower. "How the…" The only person with keys to her car was her. How had the rose gotten inside her car? She turned and looked around the parking lot. The immediate area around her vehicle was empty. Most people who had parked there at the beginning of the day had gotten there early enough that they were on their way home by now.

As she should be.

A ripple of unease crept across her skin. Roses didn't just appear inside locked cars. She reached in, picked it up off the seat and tossed it onto the dash, pricking her finger on a thorn in the process. Her cellphone rang at that exact moment. Again, she fumbled in her purse, searching for the cellphone, swearing she was going to downsize her bag to make it easier to find things.

When she finally found her cellphone and pulled it out, the phone had stopped ringing and she saw that she'd missed a call from RJ Tate. Most likely, she'd called to remind her what time dinner was.

Emily checked her backseat before she got in, something Gunny had always taught her to do. When she saw that it was empty, she slipped in, closed her door and locked it, although she wondered what good that did. Somebody had obviously gotten past her locks and put a rose on her seat. She was very regimented about locking her car door—no way had she forgotten.

Gunny had drilled safety habits into her before she had gone off to college. *Lone women tend to be targets*, he'd said. *Do everything in your power to stay safe.*

As she shifted into gear and pulled out of the parking lot, she stared at that rose once again, wondering how somebody had gotten past her lock to place that rose on her seat. It might have been cute and romantic if it wasn't completely creepy.

She drove through the evening traffic to her small apartment in downtown Colorado Springs. She liked the location because it was an easy walk to some of the nicer restaurants, and she had a great view of Pikes Peak and Cheyenne Mountain.

If she sat out on her balcony at night in the summer, she could hear music from some of the local establishments. Some people found that irritating. Emily liked knowing that people were out having fun, enjoying the company of their friends and lovers, while she preferred the quiet and solitude.

She was a good listener, and she was good at her job, but she didn't like to be in situations where she was forced to be the cornerstone of the conversation. That bookish introvert in her had gotten her through high school and college with great grades, but social situations could be challenging, except at the ranch. There, she felt at home and comfortable around Gunny and his daughter and JoJo, and the new tenants made it easy for her to sit back and enjoy the conversation without having to add too much to it.

When she arrived at home, she climbed the stairs to her apartment and tested the doorknob. It was locked, as usual. Her car had been locked, yet someone had broken in.

She inserted the key into the lock, twisted and pushed open the door. With one hand in her purse wrapped around a small can of mace, Emily entered her apartment and looked around, not sure what she expected, but she did it, nonetheless.

The apartment was small. Searching the rooms didn't take long. When she was certain no one else was in her apartment, she crossed to her bathroom, stripped out of her clothes, and jumped in the shower for a quick rinse.

As Emily stepped out of the shower, she heard her cellphone ringing. She wrapped a towel around herself and ran into her bedroom to answer it, only to discover that the caller ID was an unknown caller. Figuring it was a telemarketer, she didn't answer. If it wasn't a telemarketer and it was important, they'd leave a message.

Emily returned to the bathroom and finished drying off. No sooner had she stepped onto the cool bathroom tile than her cellphone beeped with the tone that she'd assigned to incoming voicemail. Apparently, someone did want to get hold of her and had left a message. She slipped into her undergarments, padded back into her bedroom and played the voicemail.

A voice she didn't recognize spoke in what sounded like a computer-generated voice saying, "Roses are red."

She frowned. Was that the entire message? Emily played it again. The same computer-generated voice repeated, "Roses are red."

Emily's heart skipped several beats, and her stomach knotted. The message by itself was creepy enough, but the fact that someone had left a rose on the seat of her locked car made a chill creep across her skin.

CHAPTER 2

"How was the race?" Gunny asked as he slathered barbecue sauce across the pork ribs he'd just flipped on the grill.

Cage snorted as he approached the lodge, his leg muscles so tight he could barely walk. His lungs still hurt from trying to get enough oxygen into his system at fourteen thousand feet. He was afraid to sit too long for fear he'd cramp. "Let's just say I survived."

"The altitude didn't get to you?" Gunny asked.

"I'd be lying if I said no. Running in Colorado Springs at six thousand feet isn't quite the same as running at eight to fourteen thousand feet in the mountains. I'm sore as hell, but I'll live."

Gunny shook his head. "I might have tried it when I was younger, but this old geezer just doesn't have the lung power it takes to do that race."

"You're never too old," Cage said. "There were people your age up there."

"Yeah, and I've got better things to do, like run a ranch and a bar." Gunny lifted his chin toward the lodge. "Your guys are in the basement if you want to head down there. Swede got in last night. He's doing some last-minute computer network finagling to get you guys fully operational and your computers talking to those in Montana."

"Better him than me. I only know enough about computers to check my email." Cage dipped his head toward Gunny and headed up the steps into the lodge. As he reached for the doorknob, Gunny's daughter, RJ, backed through the door with a tray full of raw meat and foil-wrapped potatoes. "You're staying for dinner, aren't you?" she asked as she skirted Cage.

He nodded. He didn't have anywhere else to go, unless he moved back into the hotel that he'd lived in down in Colorado Springs for the past two weeks while performing his separation processing. He was close to completing that task, except for a mental health appointment at the VA hospital. He didn't know why he was required to do that in the first place. Yeah, he'd been in battle, and yeah, he'd lost his friend. He was sad, but he wasn't depressed. He missed his friend, but he wasn't suicidal.

Okay, so he felt guilty that he had survived, and his friend hadn't. Wasn't that natural? Didn't most guys who'd lost buddies on the battlefield wonder why them and not me?

Jake had mentioned that one of the doors to the basement was located in the kitchen. He passed through the great room, dodged tables through the dining area, and entered the kitchen through a swinging door. As there were several doors in the kitchen, he tried the first one, but it led into a large pantry. The next one led down into the basement where he found three men hovering over various pieces of computer equipment.

When Cage reached the bottom of the steps, the others turned toward him. Jake, the former ranger who had interviewed him, straightened and approached him with his hand held out. "Cage, I'm glad you made it. How was the race?"

Cage nodded. "Long and hard."

"But you completed it, right?"

Cage nodded. There was no way he would have failed and broken his promise to Ryan.

"Did you make good time?" A tall man, with sandy-blond hair and gray eyes, approached with his hand out. "By the way, I'm Max."

"Cage Weaver." He shook the man's hand. "I guess I did okay even though I was sucking wind at the summit of Pikes Peak."

"You're a better man than I am," Max said. "I don't think that I'd want to run that race. Sounds like twenty-six miles of hell."

"I'm going to call it one and done for me," Cage said.

"Jake tells me you're a former ranger yourself?"

Cage nodded. "Jake and I served together on a tour to Iraq."

Jake nodded. "Cage saved my sorry ass once when the Taliban tried to get the better of me."

With a shake of his head, Cage corrected him. "I believe it was the other way around. You carried me out of that situation."

"Only after you shot the guy behind me." Jake glanced at Cage's leg. "I take it your wounds healed?"

Cage nodded. "I lived to fight another day because of you."

"As did I," Jake said. "Come meet the brains of this organization. I like to think of him as the computer whisperer."

"I don't know about that," said the man sitting on the floor. He rose. Straightening to his full height, he towered over the other three men in the room. His broad shoulders seemed to take up all the space, and his shock of white-blond hair made him look like a conquering Norseman. He stuck out his hand, Cage took it and the man shook with a strong grip.

Jake waved a hand toward the Viking. "Axel Svenson, meet Cage Weaver. Cage this is Swede. He keeps our computers humming and connected for all of the Brotherhood Protectors in Colorado as well as Montana. He and our main man, Hank, are the originals. Hank has entrusted me to set up and run the Colorado division of the Brotherhood Protectors."

Jake waved a hand around the room painted in subdued, natural tones in keeping with the flavor of the lodge upstairs, but lit with bright LED lights, not giving a single shadow a chance in the basement. A bank of computer monitors lined one wall where Swede had been working. "This will be our base of operations where you'll have access to the computers and certain databases that might assist you in your work. If you need additional digging or," he coughed, "special research, Swede's your guy, and he's only a telephone call or a text away. He will be returning to Montana after we celebrate our grand opening. You, me and Max are just the beginning of the Colorado team of Brotherhood Protectors. I've interviewed others and extended offers. I'm just waiting for them to get back to me."

Cage nodded toward the two doors at the other end of the room. "Is one of those the room I will be staying in?"

Jake laughed. "No, you'll have a room upstairs in the lodge." He jerked his head toward the other end of the basement. "Come with me. I'll show you what we've got." He led Cage to the first door that had a keypad and a bio scanner that matched thumbprints. Jake keyed a couple of numbers into the keypad, and then stuck his thumb on the pad. The lock clicked, and he pulled open the door.

Cage blinked at the startling array of weaponry lining the walls.

"This is our armory," Jake said. "Hank has equipped it with every kind of weapon you could possibly need to go into a wartime situation. Most of them you won't need here in the States, unless our government is overthrown, and we need to fight to take it back."

"Let's hope that doesn't happen," Cage said. "Are you sure we're not prepping for the end of the world as we know it?" Cage asked as he stepped inside the armory.

"No, but we could be deployed to other places than here in Colorado. Like I said in our interview, there might be times when we have to rescue a diplomat or a kidnapping victim from some foreign location where there are a lot of hostiles."

Cage wandered around the room, touching the smooth metal of an AR15 and the pistol grip of a Glock 9mm handgun. "And how do you plan to get these weapons past TSA?"

Jake grinned. "Hank has connections with pilots and aircraft that can get us where we need to go and back."

Cage shook his head. "Who needs the government when you have the Brotherhood Protectors?"

Jake's jaw hardened. "You'd be surprised how many people can't rely on the military or civilian law enforcement to get the job done. That's where we come in." He stepped out of the armory, and Cage followed. The other door was another storage room filled with every kind of equipment imaginable that could be used in a tactical operation, including communications devices, bolt cutters, night vision goggles, scuba gear and so much more.

Jake chuckled. "Hank wanted to make sure we didn't have a reason to decline a job."

As they came back out into the main room, Swede was just finishing putting the computer back together. "Did Hank let you know he'd be here on Friday?" the Viking asked. "And he's bringing Sadie, Emma and McClain."

Jake nodded. "I hear Kujo, his wife, and Six are coming as well. I already let Gunny know so that he could have some rooms set aside for them. We're planning on a grand opening with a few select guests who are friends of Sadie and Hank's."

Swede grinned. "That's code for potential clients."

"I hope so," Jake said. "The sooner we get to work the better."

"What are you talking about?" Max said. "You and I have already solved our first two cases."

Jake nodded. "Those were just for practice."

"And thank goodness," Max said. "Otherwise, RJ and JoJo might not be here today."

Jake smiled. "Exactly. I can't imagine life without RJ."

"Nor my life without JoJo," Max said. "We're a couple of lucky bastards."

"Yes, we are. And we proved our abilities to serve and protect others," Jake drew in a deep breath and glanced around at the basement headquarters of the Brotherhood Protectors Colorado division. "All the more reason to have this place up and running and fully connected with our base in Montana. There are people out there who need our help."

Swede shoved the computer console back under the desk and fired up the monitors. He took a seat, and his fingers flew over the keyboard. When all the monitors blinked to life with various data, Swede nodded. "We're in business."

"Yes, there are people out there who will need our particular skills to keep them safe," Max said. "Paying customers."

Jake's brow furrowed. "Something we need to keep in mind, yes. It's good when we make money, but that's not what we're all about. We're here to help people who need the help whether they can pay or not."

"I don't understand." Cage frowned. "If we don't make money, how do we afford to live?"

Jake smiled. "Hank and Sadie set up a trust fund. What money the Brotherhood Protectors make will go back into the fund, and you all will be paid out of that fund. So, don't worry; we have smart investors making sure that the fund never runs out of dollars.

That way we don't ignore the people who can't afford our services."

"I'm glad to hear it," Cage said.

Jake glanced around the room. "Now, if we're done here, there's a steak and some ribs with my name on them." He waved an arm toward the staircase. "Let's join the others."

"I could put away a steak," Swede said.

Jake laughed. "I'm betting you could put away two."

Swede patted his flat belly. "Gotta keep up my girlish figure."

Jake clapped him on the back as they walked toward the stairs.

Cage followed, and Max brought up the rear. They emerged from the basement into the kitchen where RJ and another woman were gathering paper plates, knives, forks and cups.

"Oh good," RJ said. "You guys can help." She handed a stack of plates to Jake, a basket full of knives, forks and spoons to Max and handed a pitcher full of lemonade to the other woman. "By the way, this is JoJo." RJ tipped her head toward the dark-haired woman. "JoJo, the new guy is Cage Weaver."

"Hello, new guy, Cage Weaver." JoJo set the lemonade on a counter and grabbed a tablecloth and napkins from a drawer. She stacked them on top of the basket of silverware and handed them to Max but then changed her mind, taking it all away from him. "No, better yet, you take the ice chest full of beer."

"Deal," Max said with a grin.

RJ rescued the lemonade. JoJo hefted the silverware, tablecloth and napkins and headed for the door.

Everybody had something to carry except for Cage. "What can I do to help?" he asked.

"Shoot! I almost forgot," RJ said. "There's a tray full of dinner rolls in the oven. Pull those out right now before they burn. You can carry those out."

"Roger," Cage said and went in search of an oven mitt.

"Top drawer to the right of the stove," RJ called out as she backed into the swinging door leading out into the dining room. "And the basket beside the stove is where you'll load the rolls." She held the door for the others and let it close when they'd all passed through.

Cage found the oven mitt, opened the oven and pulled out the tray of dinner rolls, setting the pan on the stove. One by one, he plucked the hot rolls from the tray and tossed them in the basket with a towel in it as RJ had instructed. In the process of moving them from the tray to the basket, he dropped one on the floor.

He muttered a curse and bent to pick it up, his sore muscles screaming in protest. The roll landed beneath the kitchen table. He had to get down on his hands and knees to retrieve the bread. As he reached beneath a chair, the swinging door's hinge squeaked, indicating someone had entered the kitchen. He assumed it was RJ coming back for something forgotten.

With the roll in hand, he straightened in time for a pretty, auburn-haired woman to run smack dab into his chest. She let out a startled yelp and stepped backward so fast she tipped and would have fallen if Cage hadn't reached out and grabbed her arms.

Her green eyes widened. "Let go of me," she said, struggling to free herself of his grip.

Immediately, he released her.

She had been leaning away from him so hard that when he let go, she staggered backward again, and would have fallen if he hadn't reached out and steadied her. This time though, he didn't grab her arms. He looped an arm around her waist and crushed her to him.

"Please, let go of me," she said, her voice shaking.

"Hey, lady, I'll let go of you as long as you can stand on your own feet. Rest assured, I'm not going to hurt you. In fact, I'm trying to keep you from getting hurt."

She stopped struggling and looked up at him. She let out a shaky laugh, her cheeks turning a soft shade of pink. "I'm okay. I can stand on my own."

He dropped his arm from around her waist and stepped back.

This time she didn't stumble. She pressed a hand to her chest. "Who are you, and what are you doing here?"

"I'm Cage Weaver, and I work here."

She shook her head. "No, you don't. Gunny, RJ and JoJo work here."

He held up the dinner roll in his hand. "Okay, so I don't work here at the lodge, but I do work in the basement."

The woman's eyes widened, and she let out a sigh. "Oh, you must be the new guy."

He smiled and nodded. "Yes, I'm the new guy, Cage Weaver."

She shook her head. "I'm sorry. Jake and Max have been talking about you. I thought tomorrow was supposed to be your first day."

"Actually, it is, but they wanted me to move in tonight. I had something to do today, otherwise, I would have been here earlier." He leaned around her and sank the dinner roll in the trash basket. "You know who I am," he said. "Do you mind telling me who you are?"

Her cheeks flushed a deeper pink. "I'm sorry." She stuck out her hand. "I'm Emily Strayhorn, a friend of the Tates."

He took her hand in a firm grip, careful not to crush her fingers.

"RJ sent me in for the tray of condiments." She tipped her head toward a collection of ketchup, mustard, steak sauce, barbecue sauce and salt and pepper.

"Tell you what," Cage said, "I'll carry the condiments if you'll carry the dinner rolls."

He grabbed the basket full of rolls off the counter, handed them to her and then collected the tray of condiments. "And, please, accept my apologies."

"For what?" she asked.

"For scaring you."

"Oh that," she said. "I'm sorry I reacted so violently. I guess I'm a little touchy."

He led the way to the swinging door and backed into it, holding it open for her. "Has something got you spooked?"

She nodded. "Just a little bit."

They were halfway across the dining room when RJ burst through the front door. "Oh, good. There you are. Everything else is out on the table. We're just waiting on you guys."

"Coming," Emily said.

Cage followed her out onto the porch where a long table had been set with enough food to feed an army.

"Hey, Cage, what do you want to drink?" Jake leaned over the ice chest, digging through the ice.

"I'll take a beer," Cage said.

Jake pulled one out of the ice and set it on the table beside several others.

Once everybody had a drink, they took their seats

at the long table and helped themselves to the food.

Cage ended up sitting next to Emily, who passed him the basket of dinner rolls. "Maybe you'd like one that didn't end up on the ground?" she said, smiling.

"A little dirt never hurt anyone. We swallowed enough of it when we ate in the field." He smiled, took a roll and passed the basket to JoJo. "You never did tell me why you were so scared?"

"Oh, it was nothing," she said, avoiding his gaze.

"Had to be something for you to be so frightened by a stranger in the kitchen."

She shrugged. "I'd rather not talk about it."

"Fair enough." Cage bit into the roll.

Jake glanced across the table at Gunny. "Who's minding the bar tonight, Gunny?"

"I got Roy Taylor mixing drinks," the retired Marine said. "The kitchen is on temporary hold until we're done here. Then RJ and I will take up the slack and see it through to closing."

Emily's eyes narrowed. "I thought you were going to hire some help?"

Gunny smiled. "I did. I hired Roy."

Emily cocked an eyebrow. "Isn't that like hiring the fox to guard the hen house? Won't he drink up all your profits?"

Gunny grinned. "He promised to pay for all his drinks out of the money he'll be making."

"So, basically, he's not going to be making any money other than the tips." Emily shook her head.

Gunny nodded. "It's only for an hour and a half."

"You really do need to hire more help."

"And I will when I find the right person. So, tell us what's going on in your world?"

She glanced down. "Not much."

Cage could feel the tension in her.

Apparently, Gunny could detect it too. "I know that look," he said.

She glanced up. "What look?"

"That look that says you don't want to bother me with your problems. Cough it up, Emily. What good is a friend if they can't help you when you need it?"

She shook her head. "You have so much on your plate now. You don't need my problems."

Gunny reached across the table and took her hand. "Emily, we're not just friends, we're family. What's bothering you?"

She chewed on her lip before answering. "I might have a stalker."

"No kidding?" RJ asked.

Emily nodded.

"How long has it been going on?" Gunny asked.

"Actually, I think just today."

"Then what makes you think it's a stalker?"

"Well, it started with a rose on the seat of my car."

RJ grinned. "You have a secret admirer."

Emily shook her head frowning. "A secret admirer doesn't break into your car to put a rose on your seat."

RJ's smile wiped clean. "Somebody broke into your car?"

"That's all I can figure," Emily said. "I lock it every morning. There's no way I left it unlocked, but when I came out this afternoon there was a rose on my seat. And there was no sign that anybody had broken a window or forced entry. How does someone get into a car that's locked?"

"The sheriff's department and the police force in Colorado Springs have tools that can get you into a locked car. Lots of people lock their keys inside. Somebody could have one of those tools and get into your car that way."

Emily shivered. "That's pretty creepy that somebody would go so far as to break into my car to leave a rose on the seat."

RJ nodded. "Yeeeah, that's kinda creepy, but it could just be somebody who likes you and wants to show you that he cares."

"I was going to give him the benefit of the doubt, until I got home, and my cellphone rang with an unknown caller ID."

"I never answer those, it's usually telemarketers," RJ said.

Emily nodded. "That's what I thought, but this one left a message." She pulled out her cellphone and played the message on the speaker. The computer-generated voice repeated what she'd listened to earlier.

"Roses are red."

RJ grimaced. "Again, it could just be a secret admirer."

"Maybe so," Emily said, "but it kind of creeps me out."

Gunny nodded. "That settles it, you're not going back to your apartment tonight."

Emily frowned. "But that's where I live."

Gunny shook his head. "And you always have a home here. You're staying the night."

"But I didn't bring anything with me."

RJ shook her head. "No excuses. You and I are the same height, and though you're a little thinner than I am, we can wear the same clothes. You don't have an animal to take care of back at your apartment, so you're staying."

"I'll think about it," Emily said.

"There's nothing to think about," Gunny said. "If you don't stay for any other reason, stay because it will give us peace of mind. If you go home tonight, we'll just worry about you."

Emily's brow twisted. "I don't want you worrying about me. You've got enough on your plate."

"Then don't make us worry," RJ said. "You're staying."

Emily sighed. "Okay, I'll stay. But just tonight."

"Yeah, we'll talk about that in the morning," Gunny said. "It's a weekend, so you don't have to go home except to get some clothes so you can come back and stay here. One of us will go with you though. You're not going alone. I never did like the idea of you living downtown all by yourself."

"I have a nice apartment, it's got a beautiful view and it's close to all of the restaurants."

"Yeah, yeah," RJ said. "And it's too far away from us."

"But it's close to my work at the VA hospital."

"True, and I understand why you want to live there. It is a bit of a drive to go through the pass every day to get to work, but you might be safer out here where you're surrounded by family and friends."

Emily smiled. "I do miss you all."

"Yes, and you're missing all the fun," RJ said. "What with the Brotherhood Protectors moving into the basement, things are about to get seriously busy around here." RJ tipped her head toward Cage. "And they just hired their third team member. You've met Cage, haven't you?"

Emily smiled.

Cage nodded. "Yes, we have. We ran into each other in the kitchen."

RJ laughed. "I hope you don't mean that literally."

Cage gave a twisted grin. "Actually, I do."

Emily laughed. "I found him crawling around on the floor after a dinner roll that escaped."

Cage raised a hand. "Guilty. I don't mind helping, but I'm a disaster in the kitchen."

"One lost dinner roll doesn't make you a disaster,"

Emily pointed out.

He nodded. "But at least now I know why you were so spooked."

She shrugged. "I didn't plan on mentioning it, but Gunny and RJ never let me get by without spilling my guts. They're the therapist's therapist."

Cage tilted his head. "So, is that what you do at the VA hospital? You're a therapist?"

She nodded. "I am. I work with veterans, trying to get them back on track so that they can live full, rewarding lives."

"Do you think that one of your patients might be your stalker?" JoJo asked.

"I haven't really had time to think about it, but yes, it could be that one of my patients left the rose and the message, but I have so many it would be hard to narrow it down. I'm just not going to worry about it unless it happens again."

"I still think you need someone to go with you back to town to get your clothes," Gunny said.

"I'll be fine on my own, but yes, I'll stay the night tonight, and tomorrow I'll go back to my place."

"I'll go with you," Cage said. "If they don't need me here."

"That's a great idea," Gunny said. "We'd all feel better if Emily had somebody go with her."

Emily raised her eyebrows. "Yeah, but if I decide to stay, how are you going to get back?"

"I'll drive my own vehicle and follow you."

Emily nodded. "Okay, but only this once. I'm supposed to be an independent woman. I shouldn't have to have my hand held going home every night."

"Yeah, and you shouldn't be getting roses and strange messages from stalkers," RJ said. "Just accept a little help graciously."

Emily laughed. "Okay." She turned to Cage. "And thank you."

Jake chuckled. "Looks like you might have your very first assignment as a Brotherhood Protector."

"He's just gonna follow me into town. He's not being assigned to me," Emily said.

Jake raised a hand. "Wait, I think I'm going to hear an echo."

Emily continued. "I don't need a protector. I can take care of myself."

"There it is," Jake said. "Isn't that what RJ and JoJo said when we assigned protectors to them?"

RJ met JoJo's gaze and nodded. "Yeah, and you were right. We needed the protection. Although we thought we could take care of ourselves. Neither one of us would be alive today if it hadn't been for Jake and Max. So, even if you think it's nothing, let Cage help you."

"Better that it be nothing and have help," JoJo said, "than it to be something and not have it."

"Okay," Emily said, "I'm convinced. Cage can be my protector tomorrow."

And just like that, Cage got his first assignment.

CHAPTER 3

AFTER A GOOD PORTION of the meal was consumed, Gunny pushed back from the table, patted his belly and sighed. "As much as I enjoy everyone's company, I have to get back to the bar."

RJ stood and started to collect the plates. "Me, too. Fortunately, we have enough steak and barbecue ribs left over we could have a special for the first ten bar patrons who lay a claim to them."

Everyone rose from the table.

"JoJo and I can take care of the dishes," Max offered.

"I'll help RJ and Gunny get the food over to the bar," Emily offered.

RJ ran inside and came back out with a roll of aluminum foil. She tore off a long sheet of it to cover the meats and handed the roll to Emily.

Emily tore off a sheet and covered the potato salad and baked beans.

Cage flipped the towel over on top of the rolls to keep them fresh and grabbed the platter of meat. "I've got this, if you'll lead the way."

RJ nodded. "Emily will show you where the bar is."

"It's easy," Emily said. "We just follow the lighted path from the lodge." She grabbed the bowl of potato salad, stacked it on top of the baked beans and led the way.

After the sun descended behind the peaks, darkness settled over the mountains. Cage studied the shadows. "Aren't you afraid of bears?"

Emily laughed. "In all the years I lived out here, I never saw one around the lodge, the bar or the barn."

"There's always a first time," Cage said.

"True." She nodded. "But actually, I've heard of more bear sightings down in Colorado Springs than up here. One of the doctors who lives in the upscale Broadmoor district caught a bear lounging in his pool one day."

Cage chuckled. "Smart bear."

"It can get hot on that side of the mountain. It's always at least ten degrees cooler up here than on the front range, usually even cooler," Emily said.

"I suppose I might need to expand my repertoire of protection services to include four-legged creatures as well as the two-legged kind."

Emily smiled. "At least we know it wasn't a four-legged creature that broke into my Jeep to put a rose on my seat."

"True, but a bear could be more deadly. Your secret admirer might only be wanting to ply you with gifts, not eat you for lunch."

RJ had arrived at the bar before Emily and Cage. She held the door open for them.

"Go on," Emily said. "We've got it." She backed into the door to hold it for Cage to bring the tray of meat through.

"It's a good thing we cooked extra," RJ said. "We've got a crowd tonight and a bunch of hungry ranch hands."

"What do you want me to do with these meats?" Cage asked.

"Gunny's got the oven warming up. You can put them in there." RJ pointed to the oven in the far corner of the kitchen.

Her father burst through the door from the bar, hurried across to the commercial refrigerator, flung the door open, grabbed a case of beer and returned to the bar.

RJ grimaced. "I better get going. Roy's behind on drink orders, and nobody's waiting the tables."

Emily slipped the potato salad into the refrigerator and poured the beans into a pot on the stove and turned up the heat.

Cage slid the tray of meat into the oven and straightened. "What can I do to help?"

"Have you ever waited tables?" Emily asked. "Or even better, have you ever served drinks at a bar?"

"No to either, but I learn quickly. I'm better at mechanics than I am at the service industry. Give me any gun, and I can break it down and put it back together in a very short amount of time."

Emily laughed. "Can you write legibly?"

He dipped his head. "Most of the time."

She fished a pad and pen out of a drawer, handed it to him, turned him around and marched him through the swinging door into the barroom. "If you can take orders and get them to the bar and the kitchen, you'll be a big help." She frowned. "Unless you're still too sore from your race today."

He drew in a breath and let it out. "At this point, I think it would be a mistake for me to sit down and put my feet up. It might be better if I just keep moving." He pasted a smile on his face and said, "So here goes." He dove into the crowded barroom. Before he got too far, RJ caught his arm and pointed to several tables, assigning them to him.

Emily smiled as she watched the former ranger fumble his way through being a waiter in a crowded barroom full of alpha men who were musky, tired, cranky and thirsty from working the fields and the cattle.

Jake entered through the backdoor. "I'll take the grill."

"And I'll help with the sides," Emily said. "And I can fill in where needed out on the tables."

RJ was back in the kitchen with several order tickets. "Get a count of steaks and ribs ASAP. I've got orders for five steaks and six ribs. Thankfully, most of them want the potato salad, but if you could get the French fries going, I know they're gonna want those after we run out of potatoes. I also have orders for a couple of hamburgers and a club sandwich."

When she'd lived at the ranch, Emily usually worked back in the kitchen where her limp didn't matter. When she got tired and her leg started aching, she'd find a stool and sit. Gunny had never pushed her too hard. She'd pushed herself, proving to be quick and efficient with her movements.

With hungry patrons wanting food fast, Emily laid out all the plates for the steaks and the barbecue ribs Gunny had warming in the oven. She placed the steaks and ribs on the plates, spooned baked beans on one side and plopped potato salad on the other. Checking the orders per table, she laid the plates onto trays along with the condiments they'd need to go with the steaks.

By then, RJ was back. She grabbed one of the big serving platters and lifted it up onto her shoulder. "Can you get the other?" she asked.

"I've got it, go on," Emily said.

She lifted the heavy tray and backed through the door into the barroom where a loud cheer went up as RJ handed around plates full of steak and barbecue ribs.

Emily smiled. Gunny's Watering Hole patrons worked hard, but they enjoyed playing hard as well. They had hearty appetites. Carrying the heavy tray made her limp more than usual. Try as she might, she couldn't keep the limp from being noticeable. She was halfway across the room when Cage caught up with her.

"Here, let me take that." He reached for the tray.

"No, I've got it," Emily said.

"Are you sure?" he frowned down at her leg. "You're limping."

She gave him a strained smile, sadly disappointed that he'd noticed. She'd never wanted to appear frail or weak in front of anybody. Especially this man whom she found so attractive. She shook her head. "If you want to help, there's another one back in the kitchen."

His frown deepened for a moment, and then it cleared. "Yes, ma'am." He disappeared into the kitchen and was out a few seconds later with the other tray.

Emily pointed to the table that he needed to take it to.

RJ met Emily at another table that the tray of food was destined for. "If you'll hold it, I'll distribute."

Happy that she didn't have to balance the tray on one hand and distribute with the other, Emily stood still while RJ quickly laid the plates in front of the appropriate patrons. When the tray was empty, RJ took it from her and loaded empty bottles onto it.

Emily spied Cage trying to do the balancing act between holding the tray and distributing plates. She hurried over to him and helped. When the tray was empty, she took it while Cage took a second round of drink orders.

Emily returned to the kitchen, stopping at the door to look back at Cage. Though he was listening to his customers, his gaze had followed her. Somehow, she had felt his gaze and did her best not to limp as she crossed the barroom, which was actually silly. What did it matter if she limped in front of this man? He probably needed to know her strengths and weaknesses so that he could better provide the protection she might need. The sooner he knew that she couldn't run, the better. Besides, he was only going to be a bodyguard to her.

It wasn't like they would be dating.

A man like Cage was strong and virile. He would date women who were equally strong and physically capable, not a bookish woman who would never consider running in the Pikes Peak Marathon.

Emily laughed. It would probably take her a week to complete the marathon, whereas it had only taken a few hours for Cage to successfully summit and return.

As she returned to the kitchen to help Jake prepare the food, she reminded herself firmly that she was alive, and she had an important purpose in life. She helped veterans assimilate into civilian society and guided them through overcoming traumatic events that kept them from resuming a full and satisfying life. Gunny had told her on more than one occasion that she'd been spared from that automobile wreck that had killed her parents and her brother for a reason. She was fulfilling that reason through her work.

When the rush for food dwindled to a trickle, Jake tipped his head toward the swinging door. "Go on, Emily. Take a load off."

"I will, after I clean up these dishes." She quickly loaded plates and glasses into the commercial-sized dishwasher and turned it on.

"Okay," Jake said as he slipped a sizzling hamburger onto a bun. "No excuses now, go."

"At least let me take that plate out to the customer who's waiting for it."

He dropped a batch of French fries onto the plate next to the burger, laid it on a small tray and handed it to her.

"What about you?" she asked. "You could use a break as well."

He gave her a crooked grin. "I'm going to clean

the grill. Then I'm going to be out there in the bar drinking an ice-cold beer."

She nodded. "That sounds good." She carried the platter out.

RJ met her at the door, took the hamburger plate and quickly handed it to the customer and set him up with salt, pepper and ketchup. She glanced around at the other patrons. "Anybody else need anything before I take a seat?" A couple of the ranch hands raised their empty beer mugs.

Gunny quickly slapped a couple full mugs on the bar.

Cage snagged them and delivered them to the thirsty customers.

RJ gave him a grateful smile. "Thank you." Finally able to breathe, she turned a frown toward Emily. "Sit."

"I'm fine," Emily said.

"You might be," her friend said and tipped her head toward Emily's bodyguard, "but Cage appears to be in pain."

Emily frowned in his direction. "What's wrong?"

Cage stopped beside her and bent to massage the back of his thigh. "Charley horse."

"Why don't you go back to the lodge and put your feet up?" Emily said.

"Not until you do," he said. "If you recall, you're my first assignment and from what little I know about being a bodyguard, I need to stick to the body I'm guarding. Where you go, I go."

Emily glanced around at the patrons of the bar. "There's still too many people here to leave RJ and Gunny on their own."

"Don't worry about us," RJ said. "We've got this. Jake's finishing up in the kitchen, and he'll be out here soon."

Emily opened her mouth about to remind RJ that Gunny had promised to hire additional staff.

RJ held up a hand before Emily could utter a word. "Don't worry. I'm working on Gunny to hire additional staff. But you know my father. He's a stubborn old man."

"I heard that," Gunny called out from behind the bar.

"That's right," RJ said. "You're a stubborn old man."

"I'll agree with the stubborn, but I'm not going along with the old. Age is just a number."

"And your number is getting higher every day," RJ reminded him.

"You're never too old to take over my knee and give you a good paddling," he warned.

RJ laughed and shook her head. "As if you ever did."

He smiled. "I thought about it a couple of times, but you and your pigtails had me wrapped around your little finger."

"Right where I wanted you," she said with a smug grin.

Emily enjoyed their banter. After RJ's mother had passed away, Gunny had taken over the reins of raising his daughter the best way he knew how, military style with a big dollop of love mixed in.

When Emily's own parents had passed away in the car wreck, they'd invited her into their little family. She knew she wasn't a blood relative, but she'd always felt loved. That fact alone had helped her overcome her grief and her loneliness. They'd helped her through physical therapy to get back on her feet and had fixed up a room on the first floor until she could climb the stairs again. RJ and Gunny had been as warm and welcoming with JoJo as well around the same time. JoJo and RJ had been best friends in high school. They'd opened their arms and their hearts to Emily, becoming the sisters she'd never had.

JoJo and Max entered through the swinging door.

"Has everyone got everything under control?" JoJo asked.

RJ nodded. "Handling it. I could use a beer."

Jake came out of the kitchen, wiping his hands on a dish towel. "Grill's clean and dishes are stacked. Where's my beer, woman?" he said to RJ.

RJ shook her head. "I'm not your waitress."

"No," he said with a grin, "but you sure are a cute one."

RJ crossed the floor, leaned up on her toes and kissed Jake. "You're lucky I like you."

He nodded with a serious look on his face. "Yes, I am. The luckiest man in this joint." He wrapped an arm around her middle and pulled her to him, kissing her long and hard.

Emily's heart swelled for RJ. She'd finally found the man for her. Raised by her marine gunnery sergeant of a father, she tended toward being a tomboy who'd rather ride horses and shoot guns than wear a dress and makeup. Not too many men appreciated a strong woman, and RJ was that. She was strong, more than just physically, and her family meant everything to her. She'd do anything for Gunny, JoJo and even Emily.

Emily always felt like she fell short of RJ and JoJo's strength. RJ and JoJo constantly reminded her that she was the smarter one of the three. Her strength was in her knowledge, they said.

Emily had always wished that it was in her muscles.

JoJo and RJ were fully capable of defending themselves.

Emily had taken self-defense lessons but wasn't completely confident that what she'd learned would work for her. She wasn't as strong as JoJo, who'd come back from the dead on her last deployment when she'd been sexually assaulted and left to die in the desert. Though she was the smallest in stature, Emily considered JoJo the strongest of all of them.

She'd had JoJo in a number of therapy sessions, helping her to overcome Military Sexual Trauma or MST. Emily smiled at the dark-haired beauty. JoJo had come a long way. The fact that JoJo trusted a man again said it all. Max was perfect for her—incredibly gentle and fiercely protective. Emily could tell that he loved her.

Her gaze crossed to Jake.

Jake had started out as a bodyguard to RJ. Max had started out as a bodyguard to JoJo. She tried to imagine the outcome of Cage being her own body-guard, and she circled back to her own weaknesses. She wasn't a strong woman. Cage needed someone who could be his partner, someone who could stand up to him and with him. Emily wasn't that person.

At that moment, Cage's gaze caught hers.

Heat filled Emily's cheeks. Thank goodness people didn't have the ability to read minds.

"Come on," he said. "Have a seat."

"You, too," she said, her voice a bit on the breath-less side.

Emily sat on one of the stools at the bar.

Cage dropped onto the one beside her, winced and groaned.

"Are the marathon aftereffects catching up with you?" Emily asked.

He nodded. "I'm afraid if I sit too long, everything's going to seize up. I'm hoping a beer will help loosen me up."

"A muscle relaxer would do a better job," Emily said.

"Maybe so," he said with a grin, "but I wouldn't enjoy it as much."

"You make a good point," she said.

Gunny wiped the counter in front of them. "What can I get you two? The drinks are on the house for my best pinch hitters."

Emily smiled at Gunny. "You know what I like."

He nodded and filled a mug with a draft light beer, placing it on the counter in front of her.

"I'll have the same," Cage said.

Gunny filled another mug and set it in front of him. "Thank you both for helping out tonight. And yes, Emily, I am going to hire some staff. Now that I have fulltime tenants with the Brotherhood Protectors, I can afford to hire help."

"Good," Emily said. "You work too hard."

"Maybe so," he said. "It helps when you love what you do."

Emily lifted her chin. "Yeah, but when was the last time you and RJ had a real vacation?"

He grinned. "What are you talking about? Here at the ranch, every day is a vacation."

Emily snorted. "You're full of it, Gunny. You and RJ are the first ones up at O-dark-thirty in the morning and the last ones to bed at night, which can also be O-dark-thirty in the morning. Do you ever sleep?" She knew the answer without him having to tell her.

He shrugged. "Sleep is overrated. Any more than six hours of sleep a night is a waste of time."

"When do you actually get six hours of sleep in a night?" Emily demanded.

Gunny's brow furrowed. "I am going to hire somebody to cover the bar at night. I'm interviewing tomorrow."

"You said that last year, and you didn't hire any of the guys you interviewed. Maybe I need to give up my job at the VA hospital and come back to work here."

Gunny shook his head. "No way. I can't afford you. Besides, you're a good therapist. The veterans need you more."

Emily glared at the man she loved like a father. "Then get on it and hire some people to help run this place."

"Yeah, Gunny," RJ said as she set her tray on the counter along with a drink order.

"I'm surrounded by pushy females," Gunny grumbled as he filled her order and pushed the tray toward his daughter.

RJ chuckled, grabbed the tray and headed back out to the floor.

"How long have you been at the VA hospital?" Cage asked.

Emily sipped her beer before she answered. "Going on three years now."

Cage smiled. "It's nice to know we have people who want to work with the veterans to help them get back on their feet." His eyes narrowed. "As young and as cute as you are, do you ever have problems with your patients falling in love with you?"

Emily's cheeks heated. "I don't," she said. "I do my very best to maintain a professional only relationship with them."

"Yeah, but some of those guys are young and easily impressionable. If a pretty girl smiles their direction, they might see that as encouragement."

Emily nodded. "I understand. Again, I try to keep my dealings with them on a very professional basis. We only talk during therapy sessions, and I never talk about myself. The less they know about me, the better. The idea is for them to focus on themselves. Besides, I'm not all that cute. They can do a whole lot better."

Gunny snorted loudly. "Cage, you hear that horseshit she's trying to feed you?"

Cage chuckled. "I don't know, which horseshit are you talking about?"

"Emily has a self-image issue. She doesn't realize just how attractive she is, and how easy it would be for her patients to fall in love with her." Gunny waved a hand toward Emily whose face burned with embarrassment. "Don't you agree?"

Cage's gaze swept over Emily's face. "I completely agree. She's very attractive."

"You two are just being nice." She tucked a strand of hair behind her ear. "I have crazy red hair, olive drab green eyes, and I walk with a limp. Now, who can find that attractive? Our veterans are used to strong, vibrant women who can easily pass a PT test, and maybe even take them down in a barroom fight."

Cage laughed. "I have known a few females like that."

"I think you're talking about RJ and JoJo," Gunny said. "But not all men want women who can kick their asses. Some guys like to be needed and prefer women who will listen to them. Someone who is smart, well-read and can carry on an intelligent conversation, like you."

If only that were true. Emily smiled at the older man. "Thank you, Gunny, you're sweet, and you're being nice, too."

"I'm not nice," he insisted. "Seriously. If I met a woman as nice and pretty as you, I'd ask her out on a date in a heartbeat."

"And when would you have time to go out on a date?" Emily asked.

"Well, there is that," he grumbled.

Emily drew in a deep breath and sighed. "Could we not talk about me?"

Gunny leaned closer to Cage, as if sharing a

secret. "And she's shy, which makes her job as a therapist even harder."

Emily pasted a smile on her face and proceeded to prove Gunny wrong, that she wasn't shy. "So, Cage, what made you decide to do the Pikes Peak marathon? Is this a one-time thing or are you normally a marathon runner?"

Cage smiled as if recognizing that she had just switched the conversation from herself to him. It was one of those techniques she used when her patients asked her personal questions. Not that Cage was a patient, but it did help deflect the conversation from her.

"I'm not normally a marathon runner. My buddy Ryan had always dreamed of doing the Pikes Peak marathon. On our last deployment, he signed us both up for this marathon, knowing we'd be back in time to compete. So, when we weren't out fighting bad guys, we must have logged a thousand running miles inside the wire of the forward operating bases where we were stationed."

"So, it was his dream?" Emily said.

Cage nodded. "It was."

Emily tilted her head. "So, who came in first?"

His smile faded. "It was a tie, but the point was we both made it."

"Will your friend go on to do other marathons?" Emily asked.

Cage looked away, shaking his head. "No, his marathon days are over."

She frowned. "Why? Did he come out of it hurting as badly as you are and decided it wasn't worth it?"

Cage shook his head. "He's not hurting at all. He just won't be doing any more marathons. Now, if you'll excuse me, I need to walk." Cage left half his beer sitting on the counter and stood. As soon as he straightened, he doubled over and cursed.

Emily got up. "What's wrong?"

"Charley horse in my thigh," he gritted out between his teeth.

"Let me help." She draped his arm over her shoulder. "Straighten your leg and pull your toe up."

He tried to straighten his leg and winced in pain. "I...can't."

"Come with me." Emily walked him toward the nearest wall. "Let's stand you up against a wall. You can press your toe up against it."

He leaned heavily on her as they both limped toward the wall.

"Now put your toe against the wall and lean into it."

He did as she said and slowly the grimace on his face eased.

RJ came up behind them and laid a hand on Cage's back. "You two should call it a night."

Emily turned to Cage. "You think you can make it to the lodge?"

He nodded.

"Go out the front door," RJ said. "The step isn't as big."

"I can handle a step," Cage said.

"Oh yeah, Ranger?" Emily asked. "Let's see you walk across the floor."

He turned, balancing all his weight on the leg that wasn't bothering him. As soon as he stepped out on the one with the charley horse, pain shot through that leg. He teetered and almost fell to the floor.

"Uh huh," Emily said, "We're going out the front door. In fact, I think we might need help from someone a little bit stronger than I am."

RJ was already on it, leading Jake back across the barroom floor by the arm. Max and JoJo had taken on the gauntlet of serving drinks to the other bar patrons.

Jake grinned. "I see that marathon just caught up with you."

"I can make it back to the lodge on my own," Cage insisted.

"Yeah, but we can't have the new guy pass out and break his pretty nose. We need you looking good for when Hank shows up for the grand opening. Come on, big guy. Suck it up and let somebody help you."

Emily chuckled. "I don't feel so bad now."

"How so?" Cage said.

"I know you'll be back up and running by tomorrow and protecting me and taking care of me. At least I can do my part now and help you today."

"This is so wrong," he said. "What good is a bodyguard who can't even stand up straight?"

"This is only temporary," she said. "Your muscles are just telling you that you over-worked them."

"You think?" he laced his words with sarcasm. It beat crying. The pain was that bad. "Fine, get me to the lodge. I'll take it from there." When he started to move his arm from around her shoulders, she held onto his hand.

"You can balance better if you have two of us."

"And I'll take the majority of the weight," Jake said.

Cage frowned. "Emily, you don't need to take any of the weight. Let Jake do the heavy lifting."

Her lips pressed into a thin line. "Why? Because I limp?"

"Well, yeah," Cage said, his brain too overwhelmed with pain receptors to think clearly about what he was saying.

"I'm stronger than you think," Emily said, her chin tilting upward. "So, quit belly-aching, soldier. Let's get you to your room." As they moved toward the door, Cage clamped his lips shut to keep from crying out. He leaned heavily on Jake but balanced on Emily through the door and out into the parking lot.

Emily smiled up at him. "See? You're not doing so

badly. Maybe by the time we get to the lodge you'll have worked that charley horse out."

"The sooner, the better," he grumbled.

A car turned on its headlights, blinding Emily.

She raised her free hand to block the glare. "Good grief, he could turn off his brights." The driver of the car revved his engine. Thankfully, they were able to move out of the parking lot onto the path leading to the lodge.

Emily glanced behind her at the vehicle with the bright headlights. Even after they'd left the parking lot, the driver remained with the bright lights shining. For someone so impatient for them to move out of the way, he didn't seem to be in a hurry to leave.

Emily shrugged and focused on getting her patient and bodyguard back to the lodge.

At a bend in the trail, she glanced back one more time. The headlights still shone toward them. They turned off and turned back on again, or had she blinked? Whatever, she navigated a bend in the trail, and the lights disappeared from view. She couldn't think about the creepiness of that set of headlights when she had Cage's arm around her shoulder making her feel things she shouldn't be feeling for a man who was just her bodyguard.

CHAPTER 4

CLIMBING Pikes Peak felt like a cakewalk compared to climbing the stairs in the lodge with a charley horse kicking his butt.

With only room for two people to ascend at the same time, Emily slipped from under the arm he'd draped across her shoulders and followed the two men up the stairs.

Cage held onto the handrail with one hand and leaned heavily on Jake with his arm looped around Jake's shoulders.

"Take it one step at a time," Jake said. "We're not in a hurry."

"Good," Cage said through clenched teeth, "because if I had it my way, I'd just pass out on a couch downstairs."

"Yeah, but you'll be a lot more comfortable in the

bed RJ's got all ready for you upstairs." Jake climbed the next step, dragging Cage with him.

Cage gritted his teeth and suffered the long climb up the stairs. When they finally made it to the top, he let go of the breath he'd been holding the entire way, while he'd been biting his tongue to keep from yelling.

Jake half-walked half-carried him down the hallway and stopped in front of a door. "This is our stop."

Emily hurried around them and flung open the door, stepped in and pulled the comforter back on the bed. She patted the sheets. "Sit down right here. I'll get your shoes."

"I can get my own damn shoes," he muttered.

Emily shrugged. "Whatever." She stepped back and allowed Jake to bring Cage over to the bed and sit him down.

Cage winced as Jake lowered him onto the mattress.

Emily waited with her arms crossed over her chest. "Okay, so go ahead and take off your shoes."

He bent forward, winced and cursed. "Maybe I like wearing my shoes to bed," he said leaning way back. "Jesus, I've had shrapnel wounds that hurt less than this."

Emily dropped down in front of him and pulled his shoes off his feet, and then stripped away the socks as well.

Cage dropped a few choice curses. "Geez, woman," he grumbled. "You're not my mother."

"Yeah, but if I were, I'd wash your mouth out with soap for all those cuss words." She straightened with a grin.

Jake laughed. "I believe I can leave you now in good hands."

Cage stared up at Jake. "I don't need to be left in anybody's hands."

"No?" He looked at Cage with a cocked eyebrow. "Do you want me to swing your legs up into the bed before I leave?"

Cage wanted to say, *No, hell no*. But when he tried to lift the sore leg, pain shot though him. He clamped his jaw closed and nodded his head. "Yes, and thank you."

Jake lifted both Cage's legs and swung them over onto the bed.

At the same time, Cage laid back on the pillow. Lying down gave him no relief whatsoever with that charley horse. He sat up again and rubbed the leg.

"If you don't need me anymore, I'm going to get back to the bar and help RJ and Gunny close up." Jake nodded toward Cage's leg. "You should be all right by morning. If not, we can see about getting a doc to prescribe a muscle relaxer." Jake glanced across at Emily. "Emily, you got this?"

Emily nodded. "I do."

Cage pressed his lips together. He hated being

beholden to anyone, especially to his new boss who he was trying to impress. "Jake…thanks for helping."

"Anytime," he said. "Just glad to have you on board."

Cage snorted. "So much for a good first impression."

"Hey, you did the Pikes Peak marathon. I was impressed. And you're allowed a little downtime." Jake left the room.

Emily fussed by fluffing up the pillows and rearranging them behind his head.

"I can take care of the pillows on my own." He sat up and rubbed his leg again.

She brushed his hands aside. "Here, let me." Her fingers smoothed over the fabric of his jeans pressing gently at first and increasing the pressure the more she rubbed. "Does that help?" she asked.

On one hand, he didn't want her massage to help, but on the other hand he did. He didn't want to be beholden to anyone, but he wanted the pain to go away. "No," he said. He really wanted her to leave him alone. He hated having her see him so weak. He was supposed to be the strong one. "I swear I've never had this happen to me before."

She laughed. "And you've never run the Pikes Peak marathon before. I'm surprised you're not coughing up a lung."

He chuckled. "I was for the first hour after the race."

Her hands continued bearing down on the muscle that was knotted in his leg. The more she did, the less knotted it felt until the pain had dissipated to the point that he wasn't wincing every time her fingers dug into the muscle.

Finally, she straightened. "Try moving it now."

He did, and it was only a little sore. He lifted it off the bed, flexed his foot and bent his knee. "Wow," he said, "I think you've cured me."

"I don't know about that, but I'm glad you're not in pain anymore."

"You and me both. I can see why your patients love therapy sessions with you," he said. "And how they can fall in love with you."

Her brow furrowed. "What?"

"A massage like that has to be the highlight of their day."

Her frown deepened. "But I…oh, never mind."

"Seriously," he said, "I can see how somebody would fall in love with you and stalk you. If your secret admirer persists, you might look through your patients' files. I could easily fall in love with somebody who could take away my pain like you just did now."

Emily's cheeks felt flushed pink. "I don't normally massage my patients' legs."

"No?" Cage cocked an eyebrow. "Well, their loss. They might recover quicker if you did."

She laughed. "I doubt that."

"Well, anyway, thank you for helping me. I hope I didn't put too much strain and pressure on you."

She lifted her chin. "I know my limits, and you didn't push them."

"I'm glad," he said. "By the way, were you born with that limp?"

She shook her head. "No. I was in a traffic accident when I was seventeen."

He nodded. "I'm sorry."

"So was I."

"Must be hard to lose full use of your leg."

She shook her head. "It's harder even to lose your family."

He reached out and grabbed her hand. "I'm sorry, I didn't know."

She looked down at where his hand touched hers. "It's okay, you had no reason to know, and it's been years."

"Yeah, but you never quite get over losing someone you care about." Now, his gaze was on their connected hands.

"Have you lost someone you care about?" she asked.

He nodded.

She squeezed his fingers. "I'm sorry."

"Yeah, me too."

She sighed. "Well, if you can handle things on your own now, I'll just be going to bed. If you need anything during the night, I'm in the room next to yours. Just yell. I'll hear you."

He held her hand for a moment longer. "Thanks, Emily. I promise I'll take better care of you as soon as I've recovered from this race."

She smiled. "No more marathons?"

He shook his head. "No more marathons."

She pulled her hand free of his and walked toward the door, pausing at the threshold. "For what it's worth," she said as she turned to face him, "I'm glad you'll be my bodyguard. At least until we can figure out who the secret admirer is and whether or not he's dangerous."

"We'll work it together," he said. "You know, we really should start with your files."

Her eyebrows dipped. "I can't share my patients' files with anybody," she said. "There are laws that protect medical information."

"Okay, so I won't help you go through the medical files. You might want to do that on your own. What about your apartment complex? Is there anyone there who's shown an interest, who might have followed you to work?"

She shook her head. "In the couple of years that I've lived in that apartment, I've only interacted with one of my neighbors, and that was a couple of months ago when she needed help carrying a large box up to her room. We keep pretty much to ourselves."

"Have you seen anyone hanging around your apartment or hanging around the parking lot at work?"

She shook her head. "No. A lot of times I'm the last one out of my department."

"Emily," Cage said, "check your patients' files."

She nodded. "I will tomorrow." She gave him a smile. "Get some rest. You put your body through hell today."

"I will," he said, "and thank you for coming to my rescue. I really haven't started this bodyguard gig off on the right foot, have I?"

She laughed. "If you recall, I didn't want one to begin with.

He nodded. "Nope, but you're stuck with me now, or at least, once I can get up on my own."

"You will," she said. "Tomorrow will be a better day." She left the room and closed the door behind her.

Someone had brought his duffle bag and his backpack up from his vehicle, for which he was thankful. When he could move again, he would need them, and it was a comfort to know that his buddy Ryan was still there with him even if only in ashes.

"What a day, huh?" he said. "You were always in better shape than I was. I'm sure you wouldn't have embarrassed yourself in front of the pretty therapist. And by the way, what do you think about her?"

He knew Ryan wasn't going to answer, but it

helped having someone to talk to, even if that someone was only there in spirit. "You heard the lady. Tomorrow will be a better day, and I promise I'll get you up to that mountain top soon. In the meantime, it's nice to still have you around."

CHAPTER 5

WHEN CAGE WOKE the next morning, he started moving, one muscle at a time. His muscles were stiff, and they were sore. But the charley horse was gone. He could live with it. He swung his legs out of the bed, grabbed his toiletry kit and headed across the hall to the bathroom.

It was early, and he hadn't expected anybody else to be in it. However, when he twisted the doorhandle, he discovered it was locked. He had just started to turn around to go back to his room and wait, when the door opened, and Emily darted out, plowing into him.

His hands automatically came up to steady her, resting loosely on her hips.

Emily planted her hands on his bare chest. "I'm sorry." Her cheeks turned a bright shade of pink as she laughed. "Why is it I'm always running into you?"

"I'm just lucky, I guess," he said.

She glanced down. "How's the leg this morning?"

"Better, thanks to you."

She shook her head. "It was just a matter of time until the muscle relaxed."

"Yes, but it never would've without you giving it a good start. For that, I thank you. I had a decent night's sleep."

"Other than the charley horse, how's the rest of you?"

He grinned. "Better. I'm sure the soreness will get worse before it gets better. I'll be okay. Okay enough that nobody else will have to carry me up the stairs."

"Good," she said with a grin. "Then you might not mind mucking stalls this morning."

He tilted his head. "Mucking what?"

She grinned. "Every time I come to stay, I do what I can to help out. Mucking stalls in the morning is one of those things. You don't have to help if you don't feel like it."

"I'm going with you," he said. "And if you're mucking stalls, I'm mucking stalls."

"Again, you don't have to. You can just watch."

"I've never been one for watching," Cage said. "I like to participate. Besides, maybe it'll help the other parts of my body loosen up some more."

"Mucking stalls takes a whole different set of muscles than running a marathon."

"I realize that," he said. "However, it's moving. As long as I'm moving, I'm not stiffening up."

"Well, if you're sure," she said, "get into some clothes that you don't mind getting dirty."

He glanced down at the jeans and blue chambray shirt she was wearing, realizing he still held her hips. He let go and stepped back.

Emily's hands fell to her sides, and she glanced down at her outfit. "RJ loaned me these. If you have a pair of boots, even better. You don't want to get horse manure down inside your shoes. The smell is hard to get out."

He laughed. "I believe spending time with you is going to be an adventure."

She looked at him with a crinkled brow. "If mucking stalls is an adventure to you, then yes. I'm headed down now."

"Do me a favor and don't leave the lodge until I'm down there with you. If I'm to be your bodyguard, I need to have your body close by."

Her cheeks turned pink.

"Strictly for protection purposes," he assured her. "I'll only be a couple of minutes. I just need to splash some water on my face to wake up, brush my teeth and I'll be down."

"Gunny and RJ have already started breakfast. It should be ready when we're done in the barn."

He inhaled deeply. "I can already smell the bacon."

"I know. My stomach is rumbling." She rested a

hand on her flat belly. "The sooner we get done out in the barn, the sooner we get to eat."

"Roger." Cage entered the bathroom, closed the door, performed his morning ablutions and hurried back across the hall to drop his shaving kit. Less than three minutes later, he was on his way down the stairs.

He found Emily in the kitchen, filling the coffeemaker with grounds. "That was fast," she said.

He grinned. "The Army teaches you to move with purpose. If you don't get things done in few seconds, you're taking too long."

"Sounds like Gunny." RJ chuckled. "He'd turn off the hot water if I was taking too long in the shower." She tipped her head toward the back door. "Jake's already out in the barn. I'd help, but Gunny and I are preparing food for some of our guests. I'll have your breakfast ready when you get back."

"Thanks." Although his legs were stiff, his muscles tight and his lungs still a little sore from pushing oxygen through his system at an extreme altitude the day before, Cage couldn't help smiling as he stepped out on the porch and inhaled the scent of evergreen. The gray dawn lit the path to the barn.

"The sun doesn't fully rise until thirty minutes after it's risen in Colorado Springs," Emily explained. "Mountain peaks block the light until the sun's rays make it over the top."

Though she limped with every step, Emily moved

pretty quickly for somebody with a bad leg. And she didn't moan or complain.

They found Jake in the barn, cleaning the second stall on the right.

"I'm finishing up this one," he called out. "There's only one other that needs work; it's across the way. You need to lead the horse out to the pasture first."

Emily smiled as she approached the stall. "Hey, Blossom," she said speaking quietly to the mare. The horse nickered and poked her nose over the top of the gate.

Emily stroked her gray nose, smiling at the animal. "That's my pretty girl." She snapped a lead on the horse's halter, lifted the latch on the gate and opened it.

Blossom stepped out and nudged her hand playfully.

"Sorry, girl. I forgot to bring you a treat. I promise I'll bring you one later."

She led the mare past Cage, tipping her head toward a wall where tools hung on hooks. "Grab a rake. There's a wheelbarrow out back."

"If it's all the same to you, I'll follow you. We can get that wheelbarrow together."

Her lips twisted. "I think I'll be just fine out here."

He walked alongside her. "Humor me. This is my first assignment. I want to do a good job."

She gave him a twisted grin. "Okay, I'm just not used to having a shadow."

"You might want to get used to it until we figure out who your secret admirer is and what his intentions are."

"I'm working on being okay with having someone dog my every step," she said. "Whether he's a stalker or a bodyguard."

He chuckled. "Wow, now you're making me sound creepy."

She glanced in his direction over the horse's nose. "You're both watching my every move. You have to agree there are similarities."

He lifted his chin and stared down his nose at her. "One big difference."

"What's that?"

"I can't write poetry," he said with a grin. "So, don't expect it."

She laughed, the sound like music in the cool morning air.

Cage liked the sound. When he figured out which direction she was headed, he hurried ahead of her to open the gate to the pasture.

Emily walked Blossom through it, unclipped the lead and gave the animal a pat on the rump. "Go on."

The horse trotted off.

Emily turned and passed through the gate again.

Cage closed and latched it behind her.

"Gunny keeps a couple of wheelbarrows on the back side of the barn. Jake has one. There should be one more back there." She led the way.

Behind the barn was a compost pile of soiled straw and a wheelbarrow that had been turned over. Cage righted the wheelbarrow and pushed it into the barn ahead of Emily.

He parked the wheelbarrow near the stall they'd be working, while Emily fetched a pitchfork and a hay rake.

Between the two of them, they had the stall cleaned out within a few short minutes. Emily directed him toward a stack of straw bales. He separated a couple of sections from one of the bales and carried them back to the stalls, spreading loose straw in a thick layer to cover the floor.

Jake appeared. "I've fed and watered the other animals. If you guys are ready, let's go get some chow."

The threesome walked to the house in companionable silence. The scent of bacon, sausage and pancakes hit them as soon as they walked through the door. Several of the tables in the dining room were occupied by guests of the lodge, who were happily eating their breakfasts Gunny and RJ had provided.

Emily waved at an older couple. "Mr. and Mrs. Daughtry, oh, I'm so glad to see you," she said and joined the couple at their table. "I forgot it was that time of the year."

Mr. Daughtry stood and hugged Emily. "We've been coming to this lodge for thirty years to celebrate our anniversary. We wouldn't think of missing it."

"I'm glad I was here to congratulate you on another year."

His wife stood and hugged Emily as well. "We just love to see you girls. We feel like you're part of the lodge family. Watching you girls grow up and become such fine young adults makes our visits here even better. How's your leg?"

Emily smiled. "It's good."

"We notice your limp is not nearly as pronounced."

"Thank you, I try."

"Will it ever go away?" Mr. Daughtry asked.

Emily shook her head. "Probably not. There was too much damage. They couldn't completely make it like new, but I'm not complaining. I can walk."

"How are things at the VA hospital?" he asked.

"Good," she said, "I love my job."

"That's always nice to see. You're a blessing to them, helping them get their lives back in order."

"I do my best," Emily said. "It's the least they deserve for the sacrifices they've made."

The older couple hugged her one more time and she made her way to the staff's table.

Emily blushed when she realized Cage had been watching the whole time. "The Daughtrys are such a nice couple," she said as she rejoined him. "They've been coming here since before I came, even before

Gunny bought the place. They were really happy when he reopened the lodge." She looked past him toward the dining room. "I'm going to see if we can help out in the kitchen."

Cage followed her. Gunny had mentioned that Emily was shy. Cage hadn't noticed. Everybody she talked to knew her, and she seemed to set them at ease as naturally as if she were born to do it. Not everybody could do that. The woman was special.

He was lucky to have her as his first assignment. She made him feel at ease just by being in the same room with him. But when she touched him, like she had last night, it made him feel a whole lot more than at ease.

If he hadn't been in pain, he might have embarrassed himself with his attraction to her. Being attracted to the woman you're supposed to guard probably wasn't a good idea. He'd have to work on that, because he'd be spending a lot of time with her until they identified her secret admirer. They were about to go through the swinging door to the kitchen when JoJo and Max entered the lodge through the front door.

"Emily," JoJo called out, "where's Gunny?"

Emily tilted her head toward the dining room. "I think he's in the kitchen."

The swinging door opened outward, and Gunny and RJ stepped through carrying trays of food. JoJo hurried across the great room and the dining room. "Gunny, we've got a problem."

"Don't tell me," he said with a grin, "you'd rather have easy over than scrambled eggs."

She shook her head. "No, we really...you need to come see this."

Gunny frowned. He and RJ set their platters on the table and followed JoJo and Max out the door. Emily, Cage and Jake were right behind them. They walked the path between the lodge and the bar and circled around to the front. Gunny swore and so did RJ.

When Cage rounded the corner of the bar, he could see why.

Someone had sprayed royal blue spray paint across the front of Gunny's Watering Hole.

RJ read the words scrawled in blue out loud. "Violets are blue."

Emily's face blanched. Cage slipped his arm around her waist and pulled her against him. "It's just paint," he said.

"Yeah," Emily said, "but he was here, and that's not just a rose. That's physical damage to somebody's property. Gunny's property."

He couldn't deny her words.

"Gunny, I'm so sorry," Emily said.

Gunny frowned. "What are you sorry about? You didn't do this."

"No, I didn't." Emily's eyes filled. "Still, I brought

him out here."

"You didn't bring him out here," RJ said. "He *followed* you, which is disturbing."

"Yes, it is," JoJo said.

"I should go back to my apartment." Emily pushed a hand through her hair. "You guys don't need this."

"Oh, sweetie, you are not going back to your apartment," JoJo said.

"You're staying here so we can all look out for you," Gunny added.

Emily shook her head. "I would hate it if something happened to one of you because of me."

"We would hate it if something happened to you because we did nothing." RJ gripped Emily's arms. "Well, it's settled; you're staying here. And there's no question now that you will have a bodyguard in Cage." She smiled and stepped back, letting her arms fall to her side. "So, stop worrying."

Emily drew in a deep breath and let it out slowly. "I'm not sure I can afford to pay him."

Jake grinned. "There's the beauty of the Brotherhood Protectors. The leader of the organization never wants money to be an issue when it comes to safety. They have a fund set up for just this situation. You don't have to worry about paying Cage."

As they studied the paint on the Watering Hole wall, Cage would have expected Emily to step out of the circle of his arm, but she didn't. If anything, she leaned even more into him.

He liked how she fit against him. She was just the right height, not too short, not too tall. He bet she would be really easy to kiss. The thought hit him before he could think through it. He was to be her bodyguard, not her boyfriend, not her date and not somebody who should kiss her. This was his first assignment with the Brotherhood Protectors. He didn't want to screw it up.

"I have a can of paint in the barn," Gunny said. "I'll get out here and paint over that this afternoon."

"No, Gunny," RJ said. "Jake and I will get out here after breakfast, and we'll take care of it. By the noon crowd, it'll be gone. Besides, you have interviews to do this morning."

Gunny sighed. "You're right. I'd rather paint the building and let you do the interviews."

RJ shook her head. "You're such a control freak, if I hire somebody, he'll be all wrong. Besides, you're a really good judge of character."

"And so are you. I didn't raise you to let bone-heads into our lives."

She smiled. "You're right, but you'll want to pick your replacement."

"Dammit, RJ, he's not going to be my replace-ment. I worked too hard to get this place where it is. I'm not just going to turn it over to somebody else."

RJ patted her father's arm. "No, you're not, but you are going to find somebody you trust who will let you actually take a day off, maybe even a whole week off so that you can go on vacation."

Gunny frowned. "I love what I do here. Every day's a vacation. I don't need to go someplace else."

"Maybe you don't, but if Jake and I decide on a destination wedding you're coming with us."

Gunny's eyes widened. "Is that what you've decided? A destination wedding? When? Where?"

RJ slipped her hand into Jake's. "After Labor Day when things quiet down here, and before the winter crowd comes in. There's usually only a trickle of guests then."

Gunny frowned. "I don't know, RJ. I haven't left this place since I bought it."

RJ planted her fists on her hips. "Daddy, you will be at my wedding if I have to have the Brotherhood Protectors kidnap you and take you there. I want you to give me away," she added softly. "You've always been the main man in my life. Now that I have Jake…"

"I'm being replaced," Gunny said. "I'm not sure I like that idea."

"Far from it," RJ said. "Now, I'll have two men in my life, and I want both of them to like and respect each other."

Gunny turned to Jake. "You already have that from me. Jake's a good man. I'll be glad to call him my son."

"Good," RJ said with a determined nod. "Then you

can do that at the wedding."

Gunny crossed his arms over his chest. "You still haven't told me where it's going to be."

"Hank's honeymoon gift to us will be to send us to Barbados," RJ said smiling up at Jake. "I've always wanted to go on an island vacation. I already live in the best place in the world. It will be fun to go someplace different. Even better, because I'm marrying my best friend, and I'll have my family around me, won't I?" She looked around at JoJo and Emily, her eyebrow hiked in challenge.

"You bet," JoJo said.

Emily grinned. "I wouldn't miss it for the world."

"Well, good, because you two are going to be my bridesmaids." Emily and JoJo converged on RJ and hugged her tight.

Cage looked on, his chest tight. These people were family. Having grown up in the foster system, Cage couldn't even remember his parents or that feeling of family, until he and Ryan had become friends. Ryan was the brother he'd never had. He'd been his friend and a confidant, and he was gone.

Emotion threatened to choke him. Even though he had held Ryan in his arms as the blood drained out of him and the light faded out of his eyes, Cage had yet to shed a tear. If anything, he was angry. Angry that it had been Ryan instead of him that died that day. Ryan was the one who was supposed to finish the Pikes Peak Marathon, not him.

They were both supposed to find the women of their dreams, settle down close by, have a couple of kids each and let them grow up together. They'd talked about having get-togethers in their backyards where they would grill hamburgers or steaks. They had tossed around the idea of taking up golf, though Ryan had moved too fast to have the patience for golf.

None of that would happen now. His friend was gone. All he had left of him was ashes. Even those, he was supposed to distribute over a mountain to fulfill his friend's dying wishes.

"Come on, our breakfast is getting cold," Gunny said.

"That's right," RJ said. "We can take care of this later."

Emily moved out of Cage's arm but took his hand instead and walked with him back to the lodge. He liked the way her fingers felt in his palm. They were strong and capable as he'd learned the night before, and yet soft and feminine. She had to be scared by the messages and gift from the stalker, but she was handling it better than he expected.

They entered the lodge and settled around the table, passing around sausage and pancakes, scrambled eggs and bacon.

"If I stay here much longer, I'm going to get fat," Emily said.

"You could stand to gain a pound or two," Gunny

said. "You've lost weight since you moved out."

"And a good thing," Emily said. "You feed me way too well."

Cage agreed with Gunny. Emily was a bit on the thin side, but she was willowy and graceful, even with the limp. Still, it was her smile and her demeanor that captivated him.

"When are you heading back to town?" JoJo asked Emily.

"I was going first thing after breakfast, but I want to stay and help paint."

Jake and RJ both shook their heads.

"Don't worry about the paint," RJ said. "We've got that. You need to go get your stuff and get back here."

Jake captured Cage's gaze. "And Cage is going with you to keep an eye on you at all times. So far, it's just been words. We don't know what your admirer has in mind next."

"Or how the rhyme is going to play out," JoJo said. "Red rose, blue paint…how's he gonna use sugar?"

Emily shook her head. "I have no idea. Something else that kind of creeps me out," she said, "is that we were busy last night at The Watering Hole. He might have been here the whole time."

"Watching you," RJ added.

Emily shivered.

Cage reached for her hand beneath the table.

Emily accepted his and held on. Her eyes narrowed. "As we were leaving The Watering Hole last night, someone was in his vehicle sitting in the parking lot with his brights on. Do you think that could have been him?"

"Did you notice what kind of vehicle it was?" Jake asked.

"No, the lights were blinding. I couldn't see past them. I just thought it was irritating. Now, I think it's creepy. At the last minute, when we turned the corner on the path to the lodge, I think the lights blinked. At first, I thought it was me, that I had blinked, but given the message on the wall, I don't know."

"Well, he's definitely watching you," JoJo said. "He had to have followed you to know you came out here."

"He also has my phone number," Emily said. "And he has access to my Jeep."

"Well, Cage knows to keep you in his sight at all times but it goes both ways," Jake said. "Make it easy for him to keep his eye on you. If you can't see him, he can't see you."

"You're used to your independence," RJ said, "and I understand that. It was hard for me to let Jake keep an eye on me. I was used to going and doing whatever I wanted. Like Jake said, you need to keep your eye on Cage as much as he needs to keep his eye on you. That way, you know you're in the same vicinity."

Emily nodded. "I'll do that, at least until we figure out who this stalker is and put a stop to his game."

CHAPTER 6

EMILY SHOWERED and changed into the clothes she'd worn the day before. She was glad RJ and Gunny had insisted she stay at the ranch. The drive into work on Monday would be longer, but she felt safer surrounded by Gunny, RJ, Jake and Cage. She wouldn't have slept if she was in her apartment. Especially after her secret admirer had left a rose in her locked car. If he was able to get inside her locked car, how easy would it be for him to get inside her locked apartment?

While Emily was combing her hair in her bedroom, Cage showered and dressed in clean clothes that didn't smell like the inside of a barn. Emily smiled. He'd been a good sport about helping to muck out the stall. Deep down, she wondered if she'd actually set him up with a bit of a test.

Some men had never been inside a barn, much

less cleaned a stall of soiled straw and horse manure. Cage took to it like he'd done it before.

Come to think of it, Emily really didn't know that much about Cage, other than the fact he'd been in the Army and he had a friend named Ryan who'd gone with him to the Pikes Peak Marathon. She'd like to meet his friend Ryan. He had to be a good guy if he was friends with Cage. She couldn't imagine Cage having anything less than a good guy for a friend.

Even though she didn't know much about Cage, she trusted her instincts about him, and Jake wouldn't have hired him if he didn't trust him completely. To be a bodyguard, the man had to be capable of protecting another person's life. Granted, her life had yet to be threatened, but based on the way the paint had been spread across the front of The Watering Hole, whoever had done it had been angry when he'd done it. That was pretty obvious. It didn't take a psychologist to figure that one out.

The question was, why was he angry? She thought back over the night. If the man had been inside The Watering Hole watching her every move, what would have triggered him to want to spray paint all over the outside of saloon?

Emily brushed the tangles out of her wet hair, her hand moving slowly as she thought through every-thing that had happened the night before inside the bar. For the most part, she'd worked in the kitchen, helping to prepare plates, out of sight of the guests in the bar.

She hadn't come out until late in the evening, at which time she'd sat down with Cage. Then she'd walked him around when he'd gotten the charley horse in his leg.

Ah, that was it. He'd draped his arm over her shoulder. To someone who was fixated on her, that might have been the trigger to make him angry. He might have considered Cage's actions as making a move on her. And her response as allowing him to make that move.

She finished her hair by pulling it back into a low ponytail at the nape of her neck. It was still wet, but she didn't care. Drying it would take too long, and she wanted to get to her apartment then go by her office and look through some of her files before they headed back out to the ranch.

Looping her purse over her shoulder, she glanced once more in the mirror. For a moment she reconsidered blow drying her hair. With it pulled back at the nape of her neck, it made her face look thin and angular, not soft and pretty. She'd forgone the makeup she usually wore on workdays. Her weekends were her days off from business clothes and makeup and dealing with other people's problems. Apparently, now, she had a few of her own.

Emily opened her bedroom door and stepped out into the hall.

Cage exited his room wearing a white polo shirt, crisp blue jeans and boots. His black hair was combed back from his forehead, damp from the shower. His blue-eyed gaze met hers. The man was so handsome he took her breath away. It made her excited to be with him all day, and at the same time, kind of nervous. Would he find her as attractive as she found him?

Cage cocked an eyebrow. "Are you ready?"

She nodded.

"We'll take my truck," he said. "Your stalker knows your Jeep."

"Good," she said. "And thank you for thinking of that."

"It's all part of my job," he said.

His words made her feel sad and her stomach knot just a little. What had she expected? She was the job, not some hot chick he wanted to take out. Obviously, what had happened with RJ and JoJo was not going to happen with her. Her bodyguard was going to work by the rules and keep it strictly professional.

And so should she.

They descended the staircase into the great room and met RJ and Jake dressed in old clothes and carrying a can of paint. A wave of guilt washed over Emily. "I really should stay and help paint."

RJ shook her head. "No way. This is gonna be fun for Jake and me. I've been meaning to put a fresh coat of paint on the front of that building anyway. The winters are pretty harsh on the paint. If we do it, Gunny won't have a chance; he's not nearly as detail-oriented as I can be, if you remember the barn fiasco."

Emily smiled. "Yes, indeed I do. You, me and JoJo ended up repainting a good portion of it because he wasn't careful with the trim."

"And his comment to us was…?" RJ prompted.

Emily laughed. "As long as it's painted, who cares?"

"But we did care, and we wanted the place to make a good first impression on our guests. With a lot of things, Gunny is disciplined and precise, but not when it comes to painting." RJ shook her head.

"I'm just glad he had some interviews this morning to keep him busy. Does anybody look promising?" Emily asked.

"He has three people lined up. His first one was a no-show."

Emily frowned. "That's disappointing."

"Yeah, but better now than a no-show when it comes time to work."

"True." At times, Emily wished she only worked part time so she could help Gunny and RJ at the ranch.

"I believe one of the applicants is a former Marine," RJ said. "Which makes me think that he will lean toward that one. And the other is prior Army."

Emily grinned. "I'm glad he likes to give the veterans a chance."

"He was specific in his ads, stating he had a veteran's preference and that bartending skills are a must."

"Is he just trying to backfill for the bar?"

RJ shrugged. "So he says. If this person is any good, I'm hoping he can take over the whole operation when we're gone for my wedding. Though don't tell him that. It's enough for him to let go of the bartending duties. Anyway, you two need to get going so you can get back."

"Don't expect us back until this afternoon," Emily said.

"Please tell me that's because you're going to do some digging in your patients' files?"

Emily nodded. "I'm going to give it a start. I really don't want to stay there all day on my day off."

"I understand. After spending all week there, you don't want to spend your weekend there as well."

Emily laughed. "Now, how would you understand that? You're here at the ranch twenty- four seven."

Jake laughed. "Emily's right."

"Hey," RJ said with a frown, "we're working on that. As soon as Gunny hires somebody for The Watering Hole, that'll free one of us up from closing."

"And when are you going to hire a cook so you're not starting breakfast before the crack of dawn?" Emily asked.

"One step at a time," RJ said. "One step at a time."

Emily hugged RJ. "You know I only want the best for you."

RJ returned the hug. "And I feel the same toward you, sister."

Emily's heart swelled with her love for RJ. "Hey, and don't forget you have to invite me when you go dress shopping."

"Dress?" RJ frowned, and then her frown cleared. "Oh, yeah!"

"Seriously, RJ?" Emily asked. "If you're planning on getting married, you kind of need a wedding dress."

"I knew that," RJ said. "We're just in the beginning of the planning phase for this destination wedding."

"And as far as destination wedding goes, whose idea was it?" Emily looked from RJ to Jake. "Yours or Jake's?"

"I know you'll be surprised to hear this, but actually it was RJ's," Jake said.

RJ grinned. "Yes, it was, and when Hank offered up Barbados, I jumped on it."

"Wow, RJ." Emily grinned. "That's really stepping outside your box."

RJ's lips twisted. "You mean the ranch?"

"I didn't say that," Emily said. "But, yes."

"Knowing that the Brotherhood Protectors are here and will help out when they're not busy doing other stuff, makes me feel better about leaving for a little while. And I have always had travel in the back of my mind. I just never had time to do it."

Emily's heart swelled for her friend. Jake would be good for her. "Well, I'm glad to see that you're changing that."

RJ held out her hand, and Jake took it. Her eyes shone as she looked up into his. "I'm just beginning to realize that life can be a broader adventure than what I've experienced so far. Don't get me wrong, this ranch has been an experience and an adventure, and it will be here when I want to come home."

"There's a whole world beyond Colorado," Jake reminded her.

RJ nodded. "I know. And I plan on seeing some of it." She turned to Emily, her smile fading. "You need to get to the Springs and back. Now, go."

Emily and Cage left the lodge while RJ and Jake headed down the trail to the Watering Hole. Cage led Emily to his truck and opened the door for her. He cupped her elbow as she climbed into the passenger seat. She liked the feel of his hand on her arm, even though she knew it probably meant nothing to him.

The drive into Colorado Springs would take between thirty-five and forty minutes through scenic vistas and a pass. It would give her time to find out more about Cage and his background. As soon as they drove off the ranch and onto the highway, she turned to him. "So, Cage where did you grow up?"

He frowned. "A variety of places," he said. His

answer was short and sweet and didn't invite a whole lot of questioning.

Emily was not deterred. She was good at figuring out other people, asking leading questions that didn't allow for a yes or no answer. "Like where?"

"Texas," he answered in two syllables.

Okay, he wasn't going to make this easy. "Any siblings?"

"No."

"What did your parents do?"

At that point he turned toward her. "They died when I was four years old."

"Oh," she said, feeling guilty for bringing up a sad or sore subject. "I'm sorry."

"Don't be." He returned his attention to the road ahead. "I never really knew them."

Even more curious now, she asked, "Were you raised by another family member?"

He shook his head.

"Foster system?" Okay, so she was digging now.

"Yes," he said and followed by a muttered, "for what it was worth."

"It wasn't a happy situation, was it?"

He gave a tight smile. "Let's just say that I got used to carrying my stuff around in a black trash bag."

Her heart squeezed hard in her chest. She could picture the dark-haired little boy being shuffled around from foster home to foster home with no siblings and no parents to call his own.

"Hey," he turned long enough to glare at her, "you asked and I answered. I don't give you permission to feel sorry for me."

Her eyes widened, and she squared her shoulders. "Okay then, I won't feel sorry for you."

"I learned how to make it on my own until I was old enough to leave the system. I joined the Army as soon as I finished high school. That's when I found out that family didn't have to be blood."

She nodded. "Your brothers in arms, like your friend Ryan."

His grip tightened on the steering wheel. Emily could tell how hard he was squeezing by the way his knuckles turned white.

"You were talking about Ryan, right?" she asked.

He nodded.

"The guy you were telling me about. The guy who ran the race with you."

He nodded again. "He was the brother I never had."

He spoke the words so softly she almost didn't hear them, but she picked up on one word, *was*.

Her eyes narrowed, and she studied him as he focused on the road ahead. "Was?" she asked softly. "Did he not participate with you on the Pikes Peak Marathon?"

He gave a laugh that held no humor. "He was with me all right. In my backpack."

She shook her head. "I don't understand."

91

"All six pounds of his ashes."

Her heart sank to her stomach. "Oh, sweet Jesus, your friend…your brother…is dead."

He nodded. "I held him while he took his last breath. Nothing else stays with you like that."

"I am so sorry." Emily stared down at her hands, feeling awful for intruding into his business. "Asking you questions about him only makes it worse, doesn't it?"

Cage sighed.

Emily sat quietly in the seat beside Cage, her heart hurting for him. The loss of his friend had hit him hard. Having grown up in the foster system… never having a family. And to find a friend who felt like a brother, only to have him die in your arms? That had to have set him back to square one. A kid growing up in the foster care system had to have issues with committing his heart and emotions to anyone. And then to do so and lose that person had to have been devastating. "How long ago?" she asked.

"Four months."

So, he was still grieving.

"Is that why you got out of the military?" she asked.

His face didn't hold any expression except for the tightening fine lines around his eyes and mouth. "My time was up. I had no reason to re-enlist."

"You weren't medically discharged, were you?" she asked.

He shook his head. "No, I'm so damn healthy it makes me sick."

"Because your friend didn't make it," she spoke the words softly.

Cage slammed his palm against the steering wheel, his face suddenly a ruddy red. "Yes, dammit. Ryan didn't make it, but I did. It should have been me."

Cage was showing classic symptoms of grief. Anger was one of the stages. "You still have Ryan's ashes?"

He nodded. "I promised I'd spread his ashes over the Colorado Rockies. I was going to do it at the summit of Pikes Peak."

"And you didn't," she said. It wasn't a question. It was a statement.

He shook his head. "Too many people. Not enough personal space."

She nodded. "It wouldn't have been right."

He frowned. "Why do you say that? Because it's illegal to spread ashes up there? I knew that. I was going to do it anyway. It was just…too crowded."

She shook her head. "No, not because it was illegal. You made a promise to your friend that you would complete that marathon with him. If you had spread his ashes on top of Pikes Peak, he wouldn't have completed the marathon with you."

He tilted his head, his brow furrowing. "You don't

think it's weird that I'm carrying my buddy's ashes around with me?"

She shook her head. "No, I don't. Not at all. It's hard to lose a loved one. It's even harder to let go, even if it is just a part of him. Some people keep urns of their loved ones' ashes in their homes. They even talk to them when they need advice or are feeling sad. It's natural."

"Thank you," he said.

She glanced his way. "For what?"

"For understanding. Most people would think I've lost my marbles by carrying around the ashes of a friend."

"Far from it. You're showing a commitment to that friend. Your love for him transcends his former physical form. I admire the fact that you want to see him through to a proper farewell."

He nodded. "Exactly." He shot a glance toward her, a real smile tugging at the corners of his lips. "Don't ever underestimate yourself, Emily."

Her cheeks heated at his warm statement. "Why do you say that?"

"You have a gift for listening."

Emily chuckled. "Why do you think I became a therapist?"

His brow dipped. "I've known therapists who barely spoke two words during a therapy session."

She frowned. "Because they were listening?"

He shook his head. "No, they came in, worked the

patient's muscles and demonstrated techniques. Besides that, they never spoke that much or asked anything other than, *Did that hurt?*"

"Good grief," she said with a laugh. "What kind of therapist do you think I am?"

He frowned. "Physical therapist, of course. I mean, what kind of other therapists are there?"

She laughed out loud. "A few other kinds."

"So, you're not a physical therapist?"

She shook her head. "No."

"But you worked the charley horse out of my leg."

She shrugged. "I've had charley horses before and rubbed the knots out of my legs. I figured that's what you needed."

His frown deepened. "Then what kind of therapist are you?"

"I'm a Licensed Clinical Psychologist. The therapy I do helps others overcome the trauma of the battlefield or sexual abuse."

He raised his foot off the accelerator, and the truck slowed. "Please tell me you haven't been psychoanalyzing me the entire time we've been talking?"

She shook her head. "No, I've been off duty all weekend."

His mouth formed a thin line. "Then why did you ask me all those questions?"

"I just wanted to get to know you, not as your doctor or your therapist, but as a friend who cares."

"Well, damn," he said. "Now, I feel like an idiot. I'm just going to sit over here and keep my mouth shut."

Emily sighed. "Please don't. Do you know how hard it is to get anybody to talk about themselves when they know that you're a psychologist?"

"I can imagine it's very difficult," Cage said. "I'm intimidated."

"I'll tell you what," Emily said, "do me the favor of giving me the benefit of the doubt. I'm not analyzing everything you say. Maybe we can do each other the favor of being friends or something." She tempered her words with a smile.

He glanced her way briefly, a smile spreading across his face. "Deal."

Traffic became more congested as they entered Colorado Springs and drove into the center of the city. Emily gave him directions to her apartment.

He pulled up in front of the building and parked.

"I'll only be a few minutes," she said and got out.

He met her on the other side. "*We* will be a few minutes," he corrected.

"That's right," she said with a smile.

"I promised to keep an eye on you. That means I'm sticking with you like glue." He offered her his elbow.

Emily hooked her hand through the crook of his arm, and they walked up the stairs together to the front door of her apartment. She took her key out and inserted it in the door lock.

Cage laid a hand over hers. "Let me go first."

She stepped back as he pushed open the door and craned her neck to see past him. As far as she could see, it appeared as if everything was normal. Her living room was just as she'd left it, with no rosebuds lying around or blue paint on the wall.

Emily let Cage lead, but she followed him as he entered the kitchen. Nothing seemed to be out of place.

He opened the pantry door; no one was hiding inside. She looked twice at the canisters she'd purchased recently that contained the flour, sugar, and rice. Something wasn't quite right, but she couldn't put her finger on it, so she ignored it and moved on. Her apartment was small with a compact kitchen, a decently sized living room and one bedroom. She followed closely behind as Cage entered her bedroom and almost ran into him when he came to a full stop, muttering a string of curses.

"What?" she leaned to the side, unable to see into the room.

"Stay here." He crossed the room and entered her bathroom. When he came back out, he pointed at the bed.

Emily took a step into the room so that she could see what had Cage cursing. She'd recently purchased a navy-blue comforter to cover her queen-size bed.

In the middle of the navy blue were streaks of white sparkling crystals. As she moved closer, she realized those white crystals formed letters making words. She read aloud. "Sugar is sweet." Her heart thrummed against her chest, and her breathing became ragged. She staggered backward. "He was here."

Cage's jaw was tight as he nodded. "Yes, he was. You might want to look around and make sure there's nothing missing or that he hasn't left any other presents. I'm calling the police." He pulled out his cell phone and dialed 911.

"I'm not gonna lie," she said. "This is creeping me out. I'm supposed to be the only one who has a key to my apartment besides the manager. How did he get in? I lock the doors. I lock the windows. Gunny drilled it into my head to play it safe. He didn't like the idea of me living downtown anyway, not alone." She trailed her hand across the top of the dresser. Nothing seemed amiss.

Cage's attention turned to his cellphone as the dispatcher answered. "Yes, I'd like to report that someone broke into my friend's apartment." He listened then gave the address. "No, the person isn't in the apartment. now. No, I'm not sure if anything is missing, but he left a message. Yes, ma'am, a message…sugar is sweet. It's not the first message he's left my friend. He's some kind of stalker. Yes, ma'am, we'll wait for an officer to arrive. Thank you." He ended the call.

Emily opened a dresser drawer. Her socks were neatly folded as she usually had them. She closed that drawer, opened the next one and gasped.

"What?" Cage stepped up behind her.

"This drawer," she said. "He's been in it."

Cage glanced over her shoulder into the drawer.

The drawer held all her underwear. Every one of the pairs of panties that she had folded neatly were scrambled and laying in disarray.

"He touched all of them." Emily shivered.

Cage slipped an arm around Emily, pulling her against him. "He might have been searching for a trophy," he said. "I've heard of stalkers taking items of clothing. Usually, the panties or bras of the women they stalk."

"I know this," she said. "I studied it in school. But this goes beyond the textbooks. It's far too close to home." She swallowed hard. "It's happening to me."

She checked the other drawers. Nothing had been disturbed in the shorts and T-shirts. She entered the bathroom and found her razor lying on the edge of the tub, not in the soap dish where she usually kept it. She lifted it and found dark stubble on the blade. She dropped the razor. "He used my razor. This guy is creepy. It makes me want to torch the entire place. I feel like my things, my space has been violated."

"Because it has," Cage said. "After the police have come and gone, you'll want to gather what you need. You're staying out at the ranch."

"I won't argue with you on that. I don't feel safe here at all." She waved a hand toward the dresser. "But I'm not wearing any of this until it goes through the washer on as hot a temperature as I can get it. I need to sterilize that bastard out of everything he's touched."

"We can do that," he said. "After the police lift fingerprints."

A Colorado Springs police officer arrived within five minutes, dusted for prints, took their statement and asked them to drop by the station to give their fingerprints so they could rule them out when they matched to the ones they'd collected.

Once they were gone, Emily grabbed a suitcase from her closet and stuffed clothes in it. The last thing she put in the suitcase were panties from her drawer. She picked them up with the tips of her fingers and shuddered as she dropped them into her suitcase. "I almost want to burn them and start all over."

"You can do that," Cage said.

"I know it's silly, and it's just clothing, but a stranger touched them." Emily trembled.

"He invaded your personal space, your safe space." Cage pulled her into his arms and held her close. "You have every right to feel the way you do."

Emily nodded and rested her forehead against his chest. "I don't like feeling...vulnerable."

"I get that." He smoothed a hand over her hair and

tipped her chin up. "I'm here to protect you. I've got your six."

She nodded. "Thank you." Then she squared her shoulders, stepping out of his arms. She placed her toiletries kit on top of the pile of clothing, closed the suitcase, zipped it, grabbed her photo album and headed for the door. "Come on, I can't stay here another minute."

She was out the door and standing on the landing waiting when he closed the door and locked it behind him. He slipped an arm around her waist as they descended the stairs and returned to his truck.

Emily tossed her case in the backseat, climbed into the passenger seat, and buckled her belt. She wasn't even sure she could ever go back to the apartment. It might be a day or two before she felt even close to comfortable going back inside. She knew she would have to soon and get the sugar off the comforter. She might even burn the comforter, although she had only bought it recently.

"Where to?" Cage asked.

"The VA hospital. I want to start going through my patient files." She gave him directions, and he headed out. She looked back at her apartment as they left. "I don't think I can ever live there again. If he got in that easily, how would I ever feel safe there?"

"Maybe once we've caught the guy, you'll feel better about it."

She shook her head. "Nope. There's no way I'll

feel safe in there again. I'm not sure I'll feel safe anywhere. The guy's been in my Jeep, he's been in my apartment, and he spray painted Gunny's building out in the middle of freaking nowhere. He knows me. He knows when I'm going to be out, when I'm not going to be in my vehicle, and when he can spray paint the outside of my friend's building without being caught. He's watching me." She shook her head. "I don't know that I'll ever feel safe again."

"Well, as long as we don't know who it is and he's not behind bars, you've got me looking out for you."

Emily reached across the console for his hand.

He took hers in his and squeezed it gently. "I've got your six. Stick with me, girl."

She nodded.

"Like glue," he said with a wink.

Emily had never been so glad to give up a little bit of her freedom for the promise of protection by a former Army Ranger. She was so thankful to have him with her she could kiss him. Oh, who was she kidding? She could kiss him even if he wasn't her bodyguard.

CHAPTER 7

THEY HAD to make a detour to the police station to record their fingerprints to make sure that the prints that the forensics team had captured were not hers or Cage's. Finally, they were on their way to the VA hospital where Emily was now even more determined to search through her files to find a patient who could possibly be behind the bizarre and frightening behavior. She had already been mentally cataloging those with whom she'd recently had one-on-one therapy sessions.

When they arrived at the VA, Emily turned to Cage. "I have a key to get into my office area, but I'm not sure I can take you in. You wouldn't make it past the security guard. He would want to see an employee identification badge since it's after hours. The best you could do is walk me up to the door, and then wait out here until I come back out. I'd hate the thought of you sitting out here in the parking lot for so long. I might be a couple hours going through the files."

Cage frowned. "You sure I can't sneak past the guard?"

She shook her head. "Even if you did, there are security cameras. I could lose my job for letting somebody in who's not authorized."

He nodded. "I understand, but I don't like you going in without me. Can we put this off until tomorrow when the hospital will be opened to the public and people have appointments?"

She nodded. "We could, but I'll be busy with those appointments."

"Speaking of appointments, I think you should cancel any one-on-one meetings for this week."

She pressed her lips together. "Some of these guys really need the help, especially the ones who've had suicidal thoughts."

"Can you conduct them virtually?"

She frowned. "I've done it in the past, and I could probably do it for the ones later in the week, but tomorrow would be too soon to organize."

"Then cancel tomorrow's meetings and rearrange the ones for the rest of the week that are individual."

She shook her head. "I hate to do that to my patients. They really need those sessions. You should be able to park yourself, not in the room with my patients, but close by. And I should be all right in my group sessions."

"I agree," he said. "Plus, you're going to invite me into that group session."

She frowned. "I could only do that if you were a patient of mine."

"Then make me a patient," he said.

"I don't know that I can do that, professionally," she said. "You and I already spend a lot of time together, which makes it hard to separate personal from professional."

"Your group doesn't need to know that I'm not a patient. You don't have to log me in. Just introduce me, and I'll blend in."

She chewed on her bottom lip.

He touched her hand. "Emily, I'm your bodyguard. I can't protect you if I'm not with you."

Her brow wrinkled. "And I can't do my job with a bodyguard in the same room with my patients."

"I can see that point with your one-on-ones, and you're probably not in as much danger in a group setting, but I want to be there just in case things go FUBAR."

She looked at him with a quizzical look. "FUBAR?"

"You know, 'fucked up beyond all repair'."

She grinned. "The military and their acronyms. I don't remember Gunny using that one. I do know that he's used SNAFU on occasion."

Cage chuckled. "'Situation normal, all fucked up.' A favorite of active-duty personnel."

"I'll have to remember that one." Emily turned her hand over and slipped it into the palm of his. "I know it's your job, and you have to follow me around, but thank you anyway for being here with me. It makes it easier and a little less frightening. Look, I'll only go in for thirty minutes and do a cursory look through my files for anyone who strikes me as a potential stalker." She laughed. "I need to brush up on my stalker personality traits, so I know what I'm looking for."

"If you have remote access to your files, you could do your search in the basement of the lodge. Swede can help you look up patient names to see if any have been arrested for any kind of violent crimes or if any have had any restraining orders against them."

Emily hiked an eyebrow. "He can do that?"

"Swede can do a lot of things."

"I thought only law enforcement officials had the ability to get into those kinds of databases."

Cage shook his head. "Jake assures me that Swede has access to a lot of things he probably shouldn't."

Emily pressed her lips together. "I don't know. I can't share the names of my patients with Swede. It would be a violation of the Hippocratic Oath and HIPAA regulations."

"Swede can get you set up, and you can do it yourself."

She nodded. "I could do that."

"And seriously, while you're in your office, cancel the appointments for tomorrow and rearrange the individual ones for the rest of the week to conduct them virtually. If you do, you can conduct those from the lodge. Swede can get you set up in a room and make it private."

"I'll think about it," Emily said. "But I do have a couple of group sessions. I can't really do those virtually."

He nodded. "And I'll be there with you for those."

"Deal," she said.

They got out of the truck and walked toward the building. When they reached the door, Cage gripped her arm and turned her toward him. "I really don't like leaving you here."

"I'll be okay. There's a security guard. If I need anything, I can call him. The VA hospital has its own police force."

"Yeah, but they can't be everywhere at all times."

"I know, but I'm sure they'll respond if I have any difficulties, and nobody should be able to get past them without an employee badge."

Cage's eyes narrowed. "Have you considered that it might not be a patient but a fellow employee, or even one of your peers?"

Her eyebrows formed a V over her nose. "I hadn't really thought about that." Her eyes narrowed and she stared into the distance. "Actually, I know even less about my peers than I know about my patients. But my gut feeling is no, at least I think no."

"Anybody you know having difficulty in their marriage? Single guys who've hit on you in the cafeteria?"

"No," she said, "I don't recall any incidents that would raise warning flags for me."

"Well, think about it," he advised. "If any of your peers are there in the hospital on their day off, be wary."

She nodded. "I will."

"And that goes for any support staff as well, like administrative support and janitors. Just be aware at all times. When you get into your office lock the door behind you."

She laughed. "For what it's worth, whoever my stalker is has been pretty good at getting past locks in cars and in buildings and he knows my phone number...my *personal* phone number. I don't advertise that anywhere."

"It's in your employee records," Cage pointed out. "Anybody with access to the employee database would know it or be able to get to it easily."

"True," she said. "Okay, I'll be careful. I'll even put a chair up to the doorknob to make sure nobody can get in. I'll have the security guard on speed dial."

"And if anybody or anything makes you at all uncomfortable, text me—I will get past the security guards."

She chewed on her bottom lip. "Now you're scaring me even more."

His face lost all humor. "This is serious business. The guy has committed two crimes already. They may not be considered violent, but it could turn that way pretty quickly."

She nodded. "Okay then, I'm going in. If I'm not out in thirty minutes…call me. I have a terrible memory."

"Give me your phone," Cage demanded.

"Why?" she handed it to him.

He brought up her alarm app and set it for thirty minutes. "No excuses. Thirty minutes."

She turned and entered the building.

Cage watched through the glass until she passed the security officer and disappeared into the elevator. He didn't return to his truck in the parking garage. Instead, he paced in front of the building. He knew he could get into the actual hospital if he wanted to go in to visit a patient, but the clinic was in a different part of the structure and the offices weren't open during the weekend. Again, he'd have to get past the security guard and potentially locked doors to go with Emily.

Fifteen minutes passed and he'd worn a hole in the grass on the lawn outside the hospital, pacing. A text came through on his cellphone. He glanced down. It was from her.

Just letting you know I'm okay. My door's locked.

Nobody's bothered me, and I haven't seen anybody in the hallways. I'll be out in fifteen.

He let go of the breath he'd held without even knowing it. She was okay. and he was worrying too much, but then he'd never been a bodyguard before, and he found that he really cared about his client. Emily was a sweet and caring woman whose job was to help people. And she did help people. She didn't deserve to be scared to go home or be alone. It made Cage angry that someone would do this to her. When he found out who was doing it, he'd...

He had to remind himself he was living in a civilian world. He couldn't take the law into his own hands for vigilante justice. But if the stalker attacked Emily, Cage would take him down without hesitation.

His thoughts went to the armory Jake had shown him on his first day. He needed to be armed. He had his conceal carry license. As soon as he returned to the lodge, he'd put on his shoulder holster, load his 9mm pistol and make it part of his routine to wear it every day. His hand-to-hand combat skills were good, but only if he could get close enough to his enemy to use them. If the enemy was armed, he'd have to be prepared to shoot him. He wouldn't have time to close the distance to use his hands to stop the guy, especially if he wasn't aiming for him but aiming for Emily. Fifteen more minutes passed, the last five with Cage watching his watch, checking it every other thirty seconds. At thirty minutes, he headed for the door, texting as he went.

Your thirty minutes is up. Where are you?

He looked up when he reached the door.

Emily was just pushing through it, wearing a smile. "I told you I'd be out at thirty minutes, and here I am."

He let go of the tension that had been mounting the entire thirty minutes she'd been out of his sight. "Come on, let's get back out to the ranch."

He cupped her elbow and led her out to the parking garage. They climbed the stairs and emerged from the stairwell. His truck was where he'd left it and everything appeared normal as they approached the tailgate, but when he reached the passenger door something looked funny about the windshield.

Emily gasped at the same time Cage realized that somebody had bashed in his front windshield. The glass was completely shattered to the point that there were shards lying on the seat in front. He muttered a string of curse words, pulled out his cellphone and called the police. While the phone rang, he looked around. Not only had his windshield been destroyed, his headlights had been smashed and the hood had dents, as well.

Emily started to walk away from him.

He grabbed her hand and pulled her close. "Stay with me."

"We need to notify the VA Hospital's police force."

"And we will, but we'll do that together."

She pointed up at the ceiling. "They have security cameras. They might have caught who did this on video."

"True." He cupped her elbow, and they walked toward the stairwell, his gaze scanning the parking garage looking for movement and not seeing any. His main concern was to get Emily out of there and into the hospital where it was safer.

They entered through the door he'd paced in front of and crossed to the security desk. The guard frowned. "Dr. Strayhorn, did you forget something?" His gaze went from her to the man behind her.

She shook her head. "No, but there's been an incident in the parking garage." She explained what had happened and the security guard notified the VA police dispatcher.

They sent one of the VA police officers to investigate. A Colorado Springs police officer arrived soon after. Cage and Emily walked with him out to the parking garage. Soon after, the Colorado Springs police officer arrived, the same detective who'd investigated the break-in at her apartment appeared.

The detective took pictures and dusted for prints, but Cage knew already that they wouldn't find any prints on the truck. They would find it on whatever tool the attacker had used to bash in his windshield and his headlights, if they could find that. The detective questioned them and made notes on the case to add to the file. They called for a tow truck and hauled the truck off to an impound lot where they would determine if there was any more evidence to collect before they would release it.

Cage notified his insurance company and arranged for a rental car to be delivered to the VA hospital where they waited. Two and a half hours after they'd arrived at the hospital, Cage drove away with Emily beside him in a rented four-wheel drive SUV. They sat in silence as he navigated traffic to get out of Colorado Springs and onto the highway toward Fool's Gold, the little town on the other side of the pass.

Once they were on the highway moving fast, Emily turned to Cage. "I'm sorry."

He frowned. "What for?"

"I'm sorry about what he did to your truck. Are you sure you want to continue being a bodyguard to me?"

"Why do you ask that?" he asked.

"It seems that your association with me makes you a target as well. For that matter, maybe I shouldn't go back out to The Lost Valley Ranch. It's made Gunny and his property a target as well. I'd feel awful if anything happened to him, RJ, JoJo or anybody else out there." She shook her head. "Take me back to my apartment."

"No way." He didn't slow down. "You're better off

with all of us, and if you ask anyone, they'd tell you they'd be willing to take the risk."

"But I don't want them to take the risk. I couldn't live with the consequences if one of them were to get hurt. They're my family. They're the only family I have. I've lost family before, and it hurts too much. Take me back to my apartment, please."

He shook his head. "I can't do that."

"So, does that mean you're kidnapping me?" she said with a smile.

"If that's what it takes," he said. "At the very least, I want to go back to the ranch because that's where I've left my weapons."

She shot a glance his way. "Wow, this is getting scarier. You think it will come to that? The use of weapons?"

"I don't know, but I want to be prepared just in case."

"Seriously," her smile faded, "I don't want to put anyone else in danger. I could just go somewhere and stay in a hotel."

"This guy's following you," he said. "He'll find you. If you're staying at a hotel, you're putting all the hotel staff and guests in danger."

"Then I'll rent a cabin in the middle of nowhere."

"You can't do that. You have a life. This guy is driving you into changing your life. You can't let him win."

She raked a hand through her auburn hair. "It's better than losing people you love."

"If you're hiding, you can't be with the people you love. You're losing them anyway."

Emily stared across the console at him. "And then there's you. I don't want anything to happen to you."

"You don't understand," he said. "I signed up for this gig. I've been in more dangerous situations than this on multiple occasions. I've been in a firefight surrounded by Taliban. This is nothing. It's one guy being an idiot. And when we catch him, everything will go back to normal."

"You might have signed up for this gig, but Gunny, RJ and JoJo didn't. I love them, they're my family."

"Then don't make their decisions for them. You already know what they'll say."

She laughed, knowing he was right. "They're not afraid of anything. I am. I can't lose my family again."

"Look, we're going out to the ranch and we'll pull everyone together and come up with a plan."

She nodded, her attention on the windshield in front of them. "Okay, but I'm adamant. I'm not going to put them at risk."

"We'll see," he said.

They drove the rest of the way to Lost Valley Ranch in silence. Every once in a while, Cage shot a glance toward Emily. She sat in stony silence, her jaw tight, her lips pressed firmly together. Her vehicle was out at the ranch. If she got it into her head that she was putting them in danger, there was a likelihood that she would take her own vehicle and leave. He'd have to stick with her like a second shadow or she'd bolt.

CHAPTER 8

As they drove up the road to Lost Valley Ranch and passed Gunny's Watering Hole, Emily looked for the blue spray paint and was pleased to see that RJ and Jake had managed to cover it with a fresh coat of paint. The Watering Hole looked better than ever. Half a dozen customer vehicles were lined up in the parking lot. Emily had no doubt that Gunny was serving his signature hamburgers and drinks to his customers.

As Cage parked the SUV in front of the lodge, Jake and RJ came out on the porch.

Emily climbed the steps to the lodge, discouraged and worried.

RJ met her at the top, a frown creasing her forehead. "How'd it go in the Springs?"

Emily shook her head.

Cage placed a hand at the small of her back, the gesture reassuring when she needed it.

"We need to have a meeting of the Brotherhood Protectors and everybody involved with Emily," Cage said.

RJ looked from Emily to Cage and back. "That bad, huh?"

Emily nodded. "Yes."

Jake's gaze ran over Cage and Emily. "Anyone hurt?"

Emily shot a glance toward Cage. "No, but Cage's truck took a hit."

Jake frowned. "What do you mean?"

Cage's jaw hardened. "Someone either took a baseball bat or a crowbar to the windshield and the headlights while it sat in the VA's parking garage."

Jake whistled. "No kidding?"

Cage's brow dipped. "That's not the worst part. The stalker left a present inside Emily's apartment."

RJ swore. "This is getting ridiculous."

"Yup. Let's get everyone together before I go into more detail," Cage said.

"I'll get Max and JoJo," RJ said. "They're out exercising the horses in the pen."

RJ left the deck and hurried out to the barn.

"Let's meet in the conference room," Jake said. "Swede's down there. He might want to bring Hank on virtually. The more heads we have in on this the better."

"Agreed." Cage liked working with a team, getting different perspectives on a problem.

"I'm going to take my things upstairs to my room for now," Emily said. "I'll meet you in the basement." She went back out to the SUV, grabbed her bag and carried it to the lodge.

Cage went halfway with her, his gaze on her the whole way as he scanned the surrounding areas and the shadowy areas beneath the trees.

If this guy knew where she was staying, he could be out there watching. He'd followed them to the hospital; he'd been at her apartment. Cage couldn't let her get too far away from him. If the stalker got close enough, he could snatch Emily and get away before Cage could do anything about it.

Cage would be damned if he'd let that happen.

Emily passed him and entered the lodge. When she started up the stairs, he followed.

She turned around with a crooked smile. "I'll be okay. I'm just going up to my room."

"Glue," he said. "I'm sticking to you like glue."

She nodded and didn't argue but continued up the stairs, carrying her bag.

When he reached for it, she pulled it away. "I can carry my own things."

He nodded and let her have her way.

Emily opened the door to her room, stepped inside and frowned.

"What's wrong?" Cage said. He moved past her

and entered the room. It looked as it had when she'd first come. The bed was made neatly, everything was in its place and there was even a nice bouquet of flowers on the table beside the bed.

A bouquet of red roses.

"Those weren't there when I left," she said, her voice shaking. "RJ," she called out. When she didn't get a response, she left the room and went to the top of the stairs. "RJ?"

A door opened somewhere below.

"RJ," Emily called out.

"Emily?" RJ's voice sounded below.

"I need you up here, ASAP."

RJ ran up the stairs. "What's wrong?"

Emily turned and led her back to the bedroom. As she reached the door, she stood aside and let RJ go in.

"What's wrong?" RJ looked around the room.

"The roses," Emily said.

"They're beautiful," RJ said. "Who gave them to you?" Then she looked back at Emily, her eyes widening. "You didn't bring those back from Colorado Springs with you?"

Emily shook her head. "No."

RJ's brow knitted. "Jake and I have been out painting the Watering Hole all morning. Gunny got busy with the lunch crowd and Swede's been in the basement all day. Do you think one of the guests might have given you those roses?"

"Let's ask," Emily said.

RJ and Emily hurried down the stairs.

"The only ones who know me are the Daughtrys," Emily said as she hurried past the empty great room to the back porch.

They found Mr. and Mrs. Daughtry sitting on the back porch in rocking chairs, drinking tea. Emily approached them with a tight smile. "Mr. and Mrs. Daughtry, there was a bouquet of roses in my room. You wouldn't happen to know how they got there, would you?"

Mrs. Daughtry smiled. "They are lovely, aren't they?"

"So, you know who brought them?" Emily asked.

The older woman's smile broadened. "Well, yes, of course."

Emily let go of the air she'd been holding in her lungs. "Oh, Mrs. Daughtry that was so nice of you."

She frowned. "No, it wasn't us. The flower delivery truck arrived a couple hours ago. They said the flowers were for you, so we put them up in your room. There was a card attached, did you not see it?"

Emily shook her head. "No, I didn't see it."

"Oh wait." Mrs. Daughtry fished in her pocket. "Oh, here it is. It fell out as we were going up the stairs. I put it in my pocket for safekeeping and forgot to put it on the bouquet. Here you go." She smiled as she handed it to Emily. "See, it says to Emily. From your secret admirer. Isn't that sweet?"

Emily's face blanched as she held the card in her

fingers. "Thank you, Mrs. Daughtry." She turned and walked away. As she entered the lodge, Cage slipped an arm around her waist.

RJ walked with her on the other side. Once they were out of earshot of the guests, RJ asked, "What does it say?"

Emily's hand shook as she tore open the little envelope. The message inside read:

Roses are blood red

Violets are blue

Sugar is sweet

And I will have you

Her hands shook so badly she dropped the note.

"I'll be right back," RJ said. She went out the back-door and was back a few minutes later. "Mrs. Daughtry gave me the name that was on the van that delivered those flowers. We can call and find out who ordered them. Maybe they have a trail we can follow, a credit card or something. In the meantime, I'll get them out of your room."

Emily gave her a weak smile. "Thank you."

RJ wrapped her arms around Emily and hugged her tightly. "Oh, sweetie, I'm so sorry you're going through this."

"I'm okay," she said.

"No, you're not," RJ said and held her at arms-length. "You're shaking like a leaf."

Emily lifted her chin. "I can handle this."

"Well, you're a stronger woman than I am. I

would be freaking out by now." RJ hugged her again. "I'm going to go get them out of your room and throw them on the burn pile."

RJ left Emily with Cage. He could tell that she was not handling it as well as she professed. He opened his arms. "Hey, you are allowed to be scared. Come here."

She took two steps forward and fell into his arms.

He held her until she quit shaking. "We're going to figure this out. I promise." He hoped he could fulfill that promise before anything happened to Emily or anybody else she loved.

Cage led Emily into the basement.

Swede sat at a computer terminal talking to somebody on the screen.

When Cage stepped up behind him, he said, "Cage, I know you've spoken with him on the phone before, but have you ever met Hank Patterson in person, the leader of this organization?"

Cage shook his head. "Not yet."

Swede tipped his head toward the monitor. "Cage Weaver, this is Hank Patterson, our boss."

Cage nodded toward Hank. "Nice to put a face to the name. Thanks for bringing me on board."

Hank grinned. "I'd like to say I had something to do with it, but Jake hired you and I trust his decisions implicitly. I understand you have your first assignment."

Cage nodded and held out his hand. Emily took it

and joined him in front of the monitor. "Hank, meet Dr. Emily Strayhorn. She's a close friend of Gunny and RJ."

Hank smiled. "Nice to meet you, Dr. Strayhorn. Swede tells me you have a stalker."

She nodded. "Yes, sir, I do. I wish I didn't."

"I'm sure," he said. "So, what's the current situation?"

"We'll fill you in as soon as everybody else gets in here," Cage said.

Hank nodded. "Well, that's good timing. I'm glad I called."

"We are too," Cage said. "We can use all the suggestions you might have to find out who this person is and stop him."

"Hopefully before Hank brings his wife and children out," Swede said.

"That's right," Cage frowned. "You'd planned on coming out for the grand opening of the Colorado division of the Brotherhood Protectors."

"Yes, and my wife has decided that she wants to come, and she has some friends there in Colorado she'd like to invite to the opening celebration."

In the next few minutes, everyone filed into the conference area of the Brotherhood Protectors. Jake and RJ entered with Max and JoJo right behind them. Gunny was the last to walk through the door.

"Who's minding the bar?" RJ asked.

"I put my customers on an honor system. What's going on?" he asked. "Emily, are you okay?"

She nodded.

"Things are just heating up and getting even closer to home," RJ said.

"Tell me about it," Gunny said.

"And by the way," Swede interrupted. "Everybody say hello to Hank."

Everyone turned at the same time and waved.

"Okay, shoot," Hank said. "What's happening?"

Cage laid it out for them from the beginning when Emily received the rose on the seat of her locked Jeep to the roses delivered to her room at the lodge. "At first it seemed like a simple secret admirer, leaving a gift of a rose and a piece to a poem," Cage said. "But now we add breaking and entering and damage to the Watering Hole."

"And pretty violent damage to your truck," Emily said.

Cage's mouth firmed into a tight line. "The dude had to be angry when he destroyed my windshield."

"He must feel like you're a threat to his relationship with Emily," Jake said.

"Relationship?" Emily said. "I haven't encouraged anyone."

"You didn't have to." RJ snorted. "Apparently, this person is obsessed with you."

"Emily," Hank said. "Swede tells me that you're a psychologist at the VA hospital."

She nodded. "I am."

"Is it possible your stalker might be one of your patients?"

"It could be," Emily said. "Right now, I haven't a clue which one."

"I understand you're regulated by HIPAA regulations, but if you have any concern that some of them might have had a criminal record related to violence, you might look at them first."

"I've only just begun going through my files."

"I can help you with background checks," Swede said.

Emily nodded. "I understand, but I can't just hand over names of my patients. It puts me at risk of losing my job and my license."

Swede nodded. "Anytime you need help mining data bases, just let me know. I'll set you up, and you can do your own background checks."

"I appreciate that," she said.

"We also understand that he sent you a recorded message. If you want to give Swede your phone, he might be able to backtrack through phone records and find out who sent it."

"Please, by all means." She pulled her cellphone out of her pocket and handed it to Swede.

"No guarantees," Swede said, "but I'll give it a shot."

"In the meantime, you need to tighten security

around the lodge," Hank said. "Jake, how's it going on hiring the two new people you interviewed?"

"Heard from them today." Jake smiled. "They both accepted the offers."

"Good to know. The sooner they come onboard the better. Swede," Hank asked, "have you got all the exterior security cameras up?"

Swede nodded. "I have, and they're fully operational around the lodge."

"You need to add them to the bar."

"Already started this morning. I should have them operational by this afternoon."

"Good," Hank said. "We need to do our best to catch this bastard as soon as possible."

Swede nodded. "And we need to do that before you, Sadie and the kids arrive."

"Agreed," Hank said. "And by the way, Kujo, his wife and baby are coming as well."

"Is he bringing Six?" Swede asked.

Hank grinned. "Yes, he is. We're all coming on the same plane."

"Good to know," Gunny said. "I'll be sure to set aside rooms."

Emily shook her head. "I can't stay here."

Hank frowned. "Why do you say that?"

"If we don't find this guy by the time your people come, I can't be here. It puts everybody else at risk. And you're talking about small children...? I'm not going to put them at risk. I'll go stay at my apartment."

"That won't be necessary," Hank said. "We'll have enough people there to protect you and our families."

"I don't feel good about this," she said. "It's me he's after, but he's impacting the people around me. I don't want anybody else hurt."

"You can't stay at your apartment," RJ said. "It's not safe."

"You have to stay here," Gunny insisted. "We won't take no for an answer."

"Wait." Emily held up a hand. "You're all making these decisions on my behalf. What about what I want? Does that even matter?"

"Of course it matters," RJ said. "But your safety is important to all of us."

"I can't stay here at the lodge," Emily stated firmly. "Staying here puts you," she pointed to Gunny and then RJ, "your Brotherhood Protectors tenants, and your guests like the Daughtrys in danger. We don't know what this guy's going to do. I can't, in good conscience, stay here and put all of these people in danger."

"Emily, you can't go back to your apartment," JoJo said. "He knows where you live. He's been inside. For all you know, he's got a key."

Emily lifted her chin. "I can change the locks."

Cage shook his head. "Not good enough. How did

he get into your apartment to begin with? He may not need a key."

"I'll go to a hotel," she said, her jaw firming.

"We've already discussed this, he'll follow you," Cage said. "Then you put the guests in the hotel at risk."

Emily's eyes narrowed. "There's got to be someplace he won't know where to look that's off the grid, that you can't follow my cellphone." Her gaze captured Gunny's.

Gunny shook his head. "Not a good idea."

Emily held his gaze. "You know what I'm thinking about, don't you?"

He nodded. "It's pretty remote."

"Not terribly. I can get there in less than thirty minutes if I go in daylight."

"You can only go there during the daylight," Gunny frowned. "I don't want you to even think about trying to make it up there at night."

Emily smiled. "So, we get there before dark."

"And you can't leave until light," Gunny added.

Cage followed the conversation between the two like following a tennis match. They volleyed words back and forth, and Cage still didn't know what they were talking about.

RJ did. "You can't be serious? Not the miner's cabin."

Emily nodded. "If I know Gunny, he keeps it clean and in good shape so it's ready for hunting season."

"I haven't been up there in a couple months," he said, his forehead wrinkling.

Emily lifted a shoulder. "So, I'll take a broom and some extra towels."

"You'll also need to take some gasoline for the generator to run the water pump."

"I'll feel better about staying there at night. We'll come down in the morning, use the facilities at the lodge and then I'll go to work."

"Seriously? You're going to go up there at night and down in the morning and then on to Colorado Springs?" Gunny shook his head. "Sounds like a lot of trouble to avoid your secret admirer."

"This isn't an admirer. He's a stalker," Emily said. "And if I'm not at the lodge at night when people are trying to sleep, hopefully, he won't bother you."

"We have the security cameras," Swede reminded her.

Emily's lips pressed together. "Yeah, and they have security cameras at the VA hospital, and yet he beat the shit out of Cage's truck, and nobody stopped him."

"Have you gotten back with the security team at the VA to ask them if they have looked through the video footage to see if they could identify him?" RJ asked.

"They promised they'd get back with me as soon as they did," Emily said. "If I haven't heard anything by tomorrow, I will check in with them in the morning when I go to work."

"You really should either call in sick or cancel your appointments for the week," JoJo said.

RJ frowned. "This guy is getting more aggressive every time. If he is one of your patients, he might hurt you during your appointment."

"Right now, I don't have any clue who it is. Maybe I need to keep all of my appointments just so I can figure it out." Emily sighed. "Otherwise, I'm just a victim waiting for the stalker's next move."

Gunny cocked an eyebrow. "In other words, you're going to set yourself up as bait? I'm not sure I like that idea."

"Not exactly," Emily said, "but at least at the VA hospital, if he comes inside, there are a lot of people around me. Cage can be close by, even if he's not in the same room with me and my patient. I can yell if I need him."

"You might not get the opportunity," Hank said.

"It's a chance I want to take. But I am not going to take the chance of somebody hurting one of you here at the lodge, so if it's okay with you, Gunny, I'm going up to the miner's cabin."

"With me," Cage said.

Emily nodded. "With Cage."

"If you're sure," RJ said. "We'll need to stock you up with supplies."

"I won't need anything but something to sleep on.

We don't plan on eating up there. I'm coming down every day to continue on with my life as usual."

"But it wouldn't hurt to take a few provisions," RJ said. "You'll need a few things in case you get stuck up there for some reason. Like maybe your ATV breaks down or something."

"Okay," Emily agreed. "But not much."

"If I recall, there are some canned goods and pantry staples already located up there," Gunny said. "You might check the expiration dates before you use them though. There should be a good stockpile of firewood already. It gets cold up there at night; you'll need to start a fire in the potbelly stove to keep warm."

Emily turned to Swede. "Swede, tomorrow afternoon when I get back from work, I would like the opportunity to tap into your computer system to do some background checks on a few of my patients."

He nodded. "Set a time. I'll have it up and ready for you."

"Thank you," Emily smiled at her family, her heart full. "Now, we'd better get moving so that we can get up there before it gets dark. If I remember correctly, that trail has some pretty steep drop offs. We don't want to get caught in the dark and miss a turn."

Gunny's mouth set in a grim line. "Maybe I should go up there with you. I know the trails better than anyone."

Emily smiled. "And so do I. RJ, JoJo and I did our

share of trail riding all over this place. Besides, the idea is to get away from you guys so that my stalker doesn't hurt you. But don't worry…Cage will have my back."

"If that's the route you're going to take," Hank said, "Jake, make sure they're well equipped with communications devices that would work."

Jake nodded. "I'll give them a SAT phone and they can take whatever they need out of the armory."

"And, Emily…" Hank said.

"Yes, sir." She stepped in front of the video camera.

"Can you fire a gun?" he asked.

She laughed. "I sure can. Gunny made sure of that."

Hank nodded. "Do you own one of your own?"

She nodded again. "I do. I keep it in my purse."

"Do better than that," he said. "Get a shoulder holster from Jake and wear it. You can forget your purse or lose contact with it, but if you're wearing a shoulder holster, your gun will be on you at all times."

"We'll set her up," Jake said. "In the meantime, we'll keep in contact with the police department and the sheriff's office and see what they come up with. Hopefully, they can get a match on the fingerprints."

"If you're all set, we'll see you guys in a few days," Hank said. "We'll be there a day early to help set up for the grand opening. Sadie's invited a few of her celebrity friends who live in Colorado to join us."

Emily shook her head. "Are you sure that's a good idea?"

"We're coming," Hank said, firmly. "And things will be okay."

"I hope you're right, for your sake as well as for your family."

Hank ended the video call.

"You don't have much time," RJ said. "Let's get your stuff together so you can head up the trail."

Emily nodded.

"Are you going to take the two-seater side by side or individual four-wheelers?" JoJo asked.

Emily would have preferred to take the side by side, but it wasn't a good idea. "We'll take the individual four-wheelers. The trails are narrow. I don't want to risk slipping off."

"Good choice," Gunny agreed. "Also, if one breaks down, you can double up and ride on the other. It's a good backup," Gunny said.

"Max and I will make sure that the ATVs are ready to go." JoJo started for the stairs.

Max followed.

RJ nodded. "I'll take care of packing up what they'll need up there as far as bedding, towels and food." She tipped her chin toward Emily. "You just need to worry about what you'll need as far as toiletries and what you want to sleep in. I'll meet you in the barn in ten minutes."

"Roger," Emily said.

The room cleared out. The only person left behind was Swede.

"Emily," Swede said.

"Yes, sir?"

"Is there anything I can be looking up? Any names I can draw on?"

She sighed. "I wish I could tell you, but my hands are tied."

He nodded. "Well, in the meantime, I'll look up names of people who've had restraining orders against them in the Colorado Springs area. I can narrow them down to find out which ones have had prior military service. I can also look at the employees of the VA hospital who might have had run-ins with the police in the past, although I don't think they would have gotten past the screening and background checks to get employment there."

"Anything you can do is better than nothing," Emily said. "And thank you. Tomorrow, I'll have a little more to go on, and I'll perform the searches myself to avoid breaking my oath."

Swede nodded. "I'll have the systems you need up and running when you get here tomorrow afternoon."

Emily glanced at Cage. "I guess we'd better get moving."

"Are you sure you want to do this?" he asked. "You don't have to go."

Emily laughed. "The hell I don't."

"I'm worried about you. If it's that dangerous on that trail, I don't want you falling off and breaking your neck."

She raised an eyebrow. "I'm more concerned about you falling off. You don't know the trails like I do. Look, as long as we go up during the daylight and down during the daylight, we'll be all right."

"What if it rains?" he said.

She grinned. "It rarely does that. It's more likely to snow before it would rain. But seriously, you don't have to go."

"And seriously, yes I do. Let's go pack for our little vacation."

She led the way, and he followed her out of the basement and up the stairs into the lodge.

Emily hoped staying in the miner's cabin would keep the others safe.

A shiver of anticipation rippled through her at the thought of being alone in that tiny cabin with Cage.

CHAPTER 9

EMILY ENTERED HER ROOM. The roses had been removed, but she could still smell their scent. It would be a long time before she liked roses ever again. Emily stared around her room, trying to think of what she needed to stay the night in a lonely cabin in the middle of nowhere with no electricity, but what the generator would provide if they chose to turn it on.

She'd need something to sleep in, if she decided she didn't want to sleep in her clothes. It was a good idea to take her pillow because anything they'd left up in the cabin would be rudimentary for a bunch of guys who just wanted to get away from it all to go hunting.

RJ would make sure that they had bottled water to take with them. They could use that to brush their teeth. Again, they could turn the generator on to run the water pump if they wanted, but if they didn't, there was a stream next to the cabin with clear mountain water that they could use to wash their faces.

She, JoJo and RJ had camped out in the cabin on a number of occasions and had stared up at the stars in the sky trying to identify constellations. She had a lot of good memories in and around that miner's cabin.

Staying there was a good plan. It was a solid plan, and it would keep her family safe by her not being there with them. It would be okay sharing the cabin with Cage because the only beds in the cabin were bunks, not that he would be interested in sharing a bed with her, but having the bunks would help keep her head on straight instead of dreaming about what it would be like to lie naked in his arms.

Heat rushed through her, coiling low in her belly. She'd be completely alone with Cage. She dug into the bag of clothes she'd brought with her from her apartment. When she'd packed, she'd been in a hurry to get what she absolutely needed and get out. She hadn't even thought about bringing a sexy night-gown. Emily sighed. It was just as well. He was her bodyguard. He wasn't interested in her as anything other than a client.

She grabbed the well-worn T-shirt she usually wore to sleep in at night and a pair of soft jersey shorts to go with them. An extra set of clothes was a good idea, just in case. Everything else she would leave in this room because she would come back the next morning, shower and get ready to go to work. She wouldn't spend more than twenty minutes in the lodge in the morning. The afternoons would be a different matter, if she planned to spend an hour or two going through the databases that Swede was going to give her access to.

Hopefully, that didn't put the occupants of the lodge at any disadvantage. Emily would only be there during daylight hours with plenty of people around to witness any attempts made by her stalker.

When she had been in her office for that thirty minutes, she'd gone through the files of her patients that she had appointments with on Monday. None of them raised any red flags in her notes. Unfortunately, people had ways of hiding mental illness. She'd keep her appointments that week unless her search on Swede's databases turned up anything that might concern her.

Besides the clothes, she grabbed the pillow off the bed, stuffed it into the bag that she would take with her, grabbed a brush, her toothbrush and headed for the door.

When she opened it, she found Cage leaning against the wall on the opposite side of the hall, holding a gym bag in his hand. "Ready?" he asked.

She nodded. "We better hurry. The sun's starting to go down. Once it goes behind the peaks, it gets dark quickly here."

He nodded and followed her down the stairs and out of the lodge. They met JoJo, Max, RJ and Jake at the barn. RJ and Max had pulled out two ATVs for their use. RJ had loaded the wire racks on the fronts and backs of each with waterproof canvas bags containing what they would need once they reached the cabin.

"You sure you don't want me and Jake to go with you guys?" RJ asked.

Emily shook her head. "That would defeat the purpose. I'm leaving so that you guys won't be targeted by my stalker."

RJ laughed. "Nobody will be targeted by your stalker up in that cabin."

"True, but it is small," Emily reminded her friend.

"Okay then." RJ stood beside Jake, her brow wrinkled. She didn't appear happy that Emily was heading up the mountain.

Jake handed Cage a satellite phone and showed him how to use it. "If you need anything, don't hesitate to call."

Cage took the phone and patted his jacket. "Thanks for this and for the pistol. And if anything happens down here, you let us know."

"We will but don't attempt to come down during the dark," RJ said. "The trails are treacherous when you can't see them."

"And a lot of fun when you can," JoJo said with a

smile. "We spent many hours up on the trails, riding all over these mountains."

Emily smiled. "Yes, we did."

"And we'll do it again," JoJo said. "We might have to bring the guys along with us because they won't want to miss out on the fun."

"Lucky you," Max said. "I've been on some of the trails, and they are a lot of fun."

"Just stay away from the open mines," Jake said. "You don't want to get trapped in one of those. They're not very stable." He pulled RJ up against him.

Max held up a hand. "I can attest to that and so can JoJo."

"All right then, we'd better get going." Emily mounted the ATV, remembering how much she'd enjoyed riding them. It was the only place she felt equal to RJ and JoJo. It didn't matter that she walked with a limp when she was riding an ATV.

"I'll get the gate," RJ said. She and Jake walked over to the gate that led out to one of the pastures, opened it wide and waited while Emily drove through it.

Cage followed behind her.

For the first time since the stalker had come into her life, Emily felt good. She felt free with the wind blowing through her hair and the rumble of the engine beneath her. She felt powerful and excited about getting up to the cabin. If she were honest with herself, much of that excitement had to do with the fact that she would be completely alone with Cage, and her stalker wouldn't have access to bother them. She could put all her worries on hold until the next day and might even get a good night's sleep.

And if she didn't get a good night's sleep, well, maybe she'd have a better reason for that than worrying about someone attacking her.

With the sun getting close to the edge of the peaks, she didn't take her time on the trail but pressed upward. At the bends in the trail, she chanced looking back to make sure Cage was keeping up.

Thankfully, he was doing a good job of it, staying back just enough that the dust didn't choke him.

The sun dipped below the peaks as they arrived at the cabin. There was still just enough light for her to make her way to the door carrying one of the canvas bags RJ had loaded onto her ATV. Cage grabbed his gym bag and the other canvas bag and followed her.

Emily flung open the door, reached inside and grabbed for the flashlight she knew would be hanging on the wall. When her fingers made contact with it, she hit the on switch. Light flooded the little room. As she shined the beam into the cabin, she paused.

"What the heck?" Instead of the two sets of bunks that used to be in the cabin there was one full-sized bed. No bunks. "I swear there were bunk beds in here." She set the canvas bag on the floor and dug into it. On the top was a hand-written note signed by RJ.

Sorry, although I'm not really sorry, but Gunny has just informed me that the bunks were removed because he got tired of sleeping on them, and he replaced them with a full-size bed. I included an extra sleeping bag in case one of you decides to sleep on the floor. If not, I hope you enjoy your stay in the cabin.

RJ

Cage leaned over her shoulder. "I'll take a sleeping bag and sleep on the floor."

"No way," Emily said. "I got you into this. You can sleep on the bed. I'll sleep on the floor."

Cage shook his head. "There's really no reason for either one of us to sleep on the floor. We're grown adults. We can share a bed. Neither one of us has to answer to anyone else. We're free, we're single, and I promise I don't hog any more of my side than is necessary. However, I do snore sometimes."

Emily chewed on her bottom lip. It was too late to turn around and drive back down to the lodge. But this was just the kind of situation she had wanted to avoid. Now she was stuck in a cabin, alone with Cage and thinking of all the possibilities of sharing a bed with him. She would not be sleeping tonight.

CHAPTER 10

Cage hadn't been completely sold on the idea of going to the cabin, with just the two of them. He liked the idea of having his team as backup. Not to mention, being completely alone with Emily could be dangerous in other ways.

He liked her. She was pretty and smart. He liked the way her auburn hair curled around her cheeks and how her green eyes darkened when she was emotional about something. And watching her slim body on the back of that four-wheeler, charging up the mountainside, made her even more attractive in his eyes.

He understood she was self-conscious about her limp, but to him her limp did not define her. Everything else about her did. Her gentle nature, the way she listened, her desire to help others and the fact that she wasn't afraid of hard work or getting dirt under her fingernails, or hay in her hair for that matter, made her more attractive than any woman he'd ever met.

He had been sensible about sharing the bed, pointing out that they were two adults capable of sleeping together without getting intimate. Once he closed the door behind them, he had misgivings. The small cabin created a deeper sense of intimacy. Maybe he should've stuck to his suggestion that he sleep on that floor. The hard wood against his back might have provided enough discomfort to prevent him from getting aroused.

Unfortunately, he'd already offered to share the bed. No strings, no touching was what he'd implied. Sleep would be difficult lying next to her when all he wanted to do was touch her, taste her lips and explore her body. The only other space inside the small cabin was a small closet-sized room that contained a tiny shower and a toilet.

Emily dropped the canvas bag she'd carried inside on the bed and turned it upside down, emptying a full-size sleeping bag onto the mattress. "If you could bring in some firewood and get a fire started, I'll start the generator, so we'll have a little water for a quick rinse off in the shower," Emily said. She plucked another flashlight out of the stuff that she'd dumped out of the canvas bag and handed it to Cage. "Just be aware that there are wolves and bears up in this area. We rarely see them but they're out there, and they're not afraid of humans."

"I'll keep an eye open for four-legged creatures of all shapes and sizes," he promised.

Cage crossed to the door and held it open for Emily. Once she passed through it, he followed her outside. Emily pointed to the right where a stack of firewood lay next to the building. She turned left to walk to the other end of the cabin where there was a lean-to shed. She opened the door and shined the light into the interior.

Cage joined her at the lean-to door and added his light, holding it while she primed the pump on the generator then flipped the switch. The generator chugged and then kicked into gear, the sound deafening in the night air. Emily left the shed door open and turned to him. "Thank you. I'll help you carry in firewood."

Together, they gathered enough logs to keep them warm for the night and kindling to help them start the fire. Back inside the cabin, they stoked the potbelly stove in the corner with the firewood and kindling. Using some sheets of an old newspaper, Cage wadded it up beneath the kindling and firewood and used a match to light it. After a few minutes, the flames caught, and the kindling burned. Before long the logs caught, and it began to warm the air inside the cabin.

While Cage had been working the fire, Emily had

spread the big sleeping bag on the bed and set out the supplies RJ had packed for them. Her friend thought of everything, including bottles of water, a small can of instant coffee, packets of hot cocoa, a box of crackers, granola bars, canned soup and instant oatmeal. Emily stacked the supplies on a shelf and glanced around.

Cage was still working the fire, poking the logs to keep them burning.

Grabbing her toiletry kit, Emily headed for the small closet-sized bathroom. "If you don't mind, I'll go first and rinse the dust off in the shower."

"Go ahead. I'll make up some of this hot cocoa."

She smiled. "That sounds good."

He found a couple of tin mugs on a shelf and rinsed them out in the sink before pouring the bottled water into a pan, which he set on top of the potbelly stove. The fire was burning nicely, and the top of the stove had gotten hot enough to heat the water. Emily liked watching him move about the cabin. His broad shoulders filled the space, making it feel even smaller.

He glanced up, catching her watching him. Her cheeks heated as she ducked into the bathroom and closed the door.

. . .

A FEW SHORT MINUTES LATER, Emily stepped out of the small bathroom wearing a long T-shirt and nothing else that he could tell.

She shivered in the cold and gave him a weak grin. "I'm sorry to say, but there's no hot water. We tend to take really short showers up here, but it's better than going to bed dusty."

He nodded. "I'll just be a few minutes. The water on the stove should be hot enough shortly to make the hot cocoa."

"I'll take over," she said. "Go get your ice-cold shower."

He grabbed a pair of his gym shorts and headed for the shower. The little shower unit was just barely big enough for him to step in and close the door and, as Emily had indicated, the water was frigid. He wouldn't be surprised if it was snow melt from higher elevations.

He rinsed as quickly as he could, glad for the chilly water to tamp down his desire. The thought of sharing the mattress and the sleeping bag for two with Emily had him hotter than the potbelly stove. The icy mountain water helped but didn't completely destroy his desire.

The image of her standing there in just a T-shirt that hung down to the middle of her thighs replayed in his mind. Just as soon as he stepped out of the cold shower and dried off, he was right back to where he'd been before he'd entered the shower—hot and bothered over his client.

He repeated to himself, "She's the client...she's the client." He was still murmuring it under his breath when he stepped out of the bathroom.

She met him with a mug of hot cocoa and a smile. "Here, this should warm you up."

When she handed him the mug, their fingers touched. That was all it took, and he was aroused all over again. Since he'd only gone in with a pair of shorts, he was as near to naked as he'd been with her since he'd met her. As well, her long legs beneath the hem of her T-shirt made him wonder how they'd feel wrapped around his waist. A groan rose up his throat. He swallowed hard to keep from letting it out. It would be a long night lying next to her and not touching her.

"Is the hot cocoa not warm enough for you?" she asked.

He hadn't even tried it. He raised the mug to his lips and sipped the sweet drink. "It's perfect," he said. His gaze met hers over the top of his mug.

She sighed. "I'm making you feel uncomfortable, aren't I?"

"I don't know what you're talking about," he said. If anybody was making him uncomfortable, it was his own lusty thoughts about the woman standing in front of him.

"Though I still think it was a good idea to come

out here and take the danger away from the people at the lodge, it might not have been such a good idea for the two of us. I mean." She stopped talking and looked to the corner of the room. "I didn't realize Gunny had changed out the beds. I had no problem with the sleeping arrangements when I thought we were coming to a couple sets of bunk beds, but now…that single bed…it's just…"

He lowered his mug and met her gaze. "Too intimate?"

"Yes," she said. "I'm sorry. I didn't realize it would be this way."

"If it makes you feel better, I'll sleep on the floor."

She shook her head. "No, I wouldn't do that to you."

"How about if I promise not to touch you?"

She laughed. "Do you think I'm afraid of you touching me?"

"Isn't that why you're uncomfortable being alone with me here?"

She shook her head. "No, it's completely the opposite."

"I don't understand," he said.

"I'm not afraid of you touching me. If anything, I'm afraid of you *not* touching me." Her voice lowered to a whisper. "I'm afraid I won't be able to keep my hands off you."

Cage's pulse picked up, sending heat and adrenaline throughout his body and pooling low in his groin. "You're afraid I won't want to touch you?" He set his mug on the small table, took hers from her hands and sat it next to his. Then he took her hand and pulled her close, wrapping his arm around her waist. "You're afraid I won't want to touch you?" he asked again.

She nodded, staring up into his eyes, her hands resting on his chest.

"Sweetheart," he said, "I've wanted to touch you since the moment I met you."

She looked up at him, her eyes wide. "Why?"

He chuckled. "I find you completely attractive."

"But I'm not," Emily said.

"For a smart woman who has more brains in her little finger than I have in my head, you can be completely clueless." He pulled her closer and bent his head toward her until his lips hovered over hers. "You are a beautiful woman." She started to shake her head, so he lowered his lips to cover hers. He brushed against them gently then raised his head. "I can imagine every one of your male patients are already in love with you, and I might just be halfway there myself."

"Oh, please," she said. "You don't have to pretend to like me just because I'm your client."

He leaned back and stared into her eyes. "You really don't understand, do you?"

"No," she said. "All I know is that I find you extremely attractive, and I've wanted to rub my fingers over your naked skin." Her hands slid across his chest and downward until they found his hard brown nipples. She circled them with her fingertips. "You're such a dichotomy of sensations with your smooth skin and hard muscles. I don't think I could sleep with you and not want to touch you." She frowned up at him. "I really didn't bring you up here to take advantage of you."

He laughed out loud. "Please," he said, "take advantage of me, because I plan to do the same with you." Cage gathered Emily in his arms.

With her hands still resting lightly on his chest, she met his gaze, her green eyes glowing in the light from the lantern she'd found in a corner. "I want you to know I have no expectations for anything beyond tonight. No strings, no commitment, no requirement to pledge our undying love." She laughed. "We barely know each other."

"I know enough about you to know I'm attracted to you," Cage said. "I'm pretty sure what I want to do with you goes against everything inside the bodyguard rulebook for dummies. The first page states in bold letters, *Don't make love to your client.*"

Emily nodded. "What we're considering is probably wrong in every way."

"Absolutely." Cage grinned. "Are you trying to talk me out of it?"

Emily's lips curved upward in a tentative smile. "No. Not in the least. The problem is that I've always been the rule-follower, doing what my parents would have expected from me as the oldest child. Even after they died, I could hear their voices in the back of my head, guiding me to do all the right things. And there was the side of me that wanted to please my new family by keeping my nose clean, making good grades and realizing my full potential. I felt obligated to be the good girl."

Cage frowned. "So, does this make you uncomfortable? Being alone with me?"

"Yes, it does. In the best way imaginable." Emily leaned up on her toes and pressed her lips to his. "I've learned in the last twenty-four hours that being a good girl doesn't make you any less of a target. It doesn't pay to be nice."

"Yeah, but if you weren't nice—" he lowered his head until his lips hovered over hers, "you wouldn't be the person you are." He tucked a lock of her auburn hair behind her ear. "I'm really surprised you don't have more of a temper than you do. Aren't redheads notorious for their fiery tempers?"

"Maybe my fire is not in my temper." She glanced at him from beneath hooded eyes. "Perhaps if I weren't so nice, I wouldn't have encouraged someone to stalk me." She closed her eyes and shook her head. "Tonight, it doesn't matter. The stalker hasn't caught up to me. He can't find me here. I want to take full advantage of the solitude and safety...and you." She smiled up at him.

He cupped her cheek with his palm and whispered, "Are you sure about this? Are you sure this is what you want?"

Emily nodded, turned her face into his palm and pressed her lips to his lifeline. "I'm sure. I want to forget everything that has happened over the past twenty-four hours. I want to pretend you and I are the last man and woman left on the planet. Just you and me."

He bent, scooped her up in his arms and carried her the one step it took to get to the bed where she'd laid out the sleeping bag for two.

She stared up at him. "I don't suppose you brought protection?"

He smiled. "I never leave home without it." He reached into his bag, pulled out his shaving kit and dug out a packet from inside.

"Always prepared?" she asked.

"I put it in there a while back when I went on vacation. I never met anyone I felt drawn to." He bent over her and kissed her lips. "Until you."

She wound her arms around his neck and deepened the kiss, opening to let him sweep past her teeth to caress her tongue with his. The more he kissed her, the more he wanted to. Finally, he lifted his head. "Anytime you feel uncomfortable with anything we do, you tell me. I'll stop."

Emily tightened her hold around his neck, pulling

him the rest of the way down on top of her. "Don't stop. I want whatever you have to give."

Heat swept through him, carried by his racing pulse to every part of his body. In that moment, in that cabin on a mountain in the middle of nowhere, he was going to make love to a woman who set his soul on fire. "Sweetheart, I'm yours."

EMILY RAN her hands over Cage's chest and across his shoulders, loving the feel of his hard muscles and smooth skin. She couldn't wait to feel his body against hers. Skin to skin. When she reached for the hem of her shirt, he brushed her hands aside and slid his up beneath the fabric to capture her breasts in the palms of his hands.

Emily arched her back, pressing into his hands. Still, there was the matter of her shirt between them. It was too much.

Then his hands left her breasts and trailed over her ribs and down to the hem of her shirt. He held onto the fabric and dragged it up her torso over her breasts. Pausing at that point, he captured a nipple between his lips and flicked the tip with his tongue until Emily moaned aloud. The sound echoed in the small cabin, adding to the erotic vibe of lying on a sleeping bag with a fire blazing in the stove, warming the cabin's interior.

Cage switched to the other breast and sucked it

into his mouth, teasing the hardening bud with his tongue, rolling it around between his teeth.

She clutched his head to her, wanting him to keep doing what he was doing.

Alas, he abandoned her breasts, tugged her T-shirt higher until she raised her arms over her head, and he divested her of the garment. Then he returned his lips to take one of her nipples, swirling his tongue around and around until she took matters into her own hands and directed his hand to the juncture of her thighs.

He chuckled. "What's the matter?"

"Not moving nearly fast enough," she said through gritted teeth. If she didn't have him inside her soon, she would come apart. Hell, she was likely to come apart anyway with the way his skin felt against hers.

Cage cupped her sex and pressed a finger into her entrance. A burst of fire washed over her. She raised her hips from the bed, urging him deeper.

Her breathing became erratic, and her pulse hammered through her veins.

Cage trailed kisses down her torso, converging on the path his hand had taken. He parted her folds and touched his tongue to her clit.

Her breath arrested in her lungs as explosions of sensation shot out from her center. It was hot and intense and building with each passing second.

He touched her again with his tongue, flicking the

bundle of nerves until she grabbed his hair and held him there. On the one hand, she wasn't sure she could take much more. On the other hand, she couldn't let him stop. Not when she was so close to losing it altogether.

Cage pressed a finger into her channel, then added another and yet another, stretching her entrance while swirling and pumping. All the while, he licked her clit until she reached the edge of the world and rocketed into the stratosphere.

Her hips rocked to the rhythm of her release as she rode the wave all the way to the end.

Cage continued to strum her like a musical instrument until she collapsed against the mattress, breathing hard, sated but not finished.

She tightened her hold on his hair and dragged him up her body.

He chuckled. "That hair is attached to my scalp."

"Shut up and make love to me," she said through tight lips. "I want you. Now. Inside me."

"Yes, ma'am," he murmured. Then he grabbed for the packet he'd unearthed from his shaving kit, tore it open and rolled protection down over his engorged cock.

Emily gripped his hips and guided him to her entrance.

Leaning over her, he kissed her and slid into her warm, slick channel.

He felt so good, so thick and hard, he took her breath away.

When he sank as deep as he could go, he held steady, his jaw tight, his face tense, allowing her to stretch and accommodate his size.

Impatient for more, Emily pushed his hips, forcing him to slide out almost to the tip of his cock, then she brought him back in. Soon he set the pace, rocking in and out of her, increasing the speed until he pumped like a piston in a race car.

Emily raised her hips, meeting his thrusts until that tingling started at her center and ricocheted through her nerves out to the very tips of her fingers and toes. She cried out in her release.

Cage's body tensed, and he slammed into her one last time, driving as deeply as he could go. Then he stopped, his shaft throbbing against her channel as he came.

For a long moment, he leaned over her, his head thrown back, his face tight with concentration. Then he collapsed on top of her, kissed her hard and rolled with her onto their sides, dragging in deep breaths to fill his lungs.

They maintained their intimate connection, Emily draping her leg over Cage's thigh, loving that they were lying naked in a cabin with no one there spying on them or interrupting what had been the best sex Emily had ever had.

"Wow," she said and gave a shaky laugh.

"Yeah." Cage chuckled. "Wow."

"I didn't expect it to be that good," she said and immediately wished the words back.

Cage burst out laughing. "Did you not think I had it in me to make you come?"

She shook her head her eyes wide. "No. I didn't think I'd have what it takes to get you all the way there."

"For a smart woman, you can be clueless. You're a beautiful woman, and you totally turn me on." His brow twisted. "In case you hadn't noticed, I came far too quickly. Next time, I'll take it a little slower."

"Next time?" Emily asked. "Mmm. That sounds nice."

Cage swept a strand of her hair back from her forehead and smiled. "What happened to no expectations?"

"I won't hold you to anything, but I have to admit, I've had a change of heart."

"You don't want to have a next time?"

"On the contrary, I want a lot more next times, starting as soon as you've recuperated from this time." She grinned and felt him thickening inside her. "I can see that sleep will not be a high priority tonight. And I'm perfectly okay with that. We can sleep when we're dead."

"Whoa, sweetheart." He cupped her jaw and pressed a kiss to her lips. "Don't say things like that.

I'd hate for anything to happen to you now that I've found you."

Feeling powerful, Emily wrapped her arms around him, rolled him onto his back and straddled his hips. "Same here. What's your stance on women on top?"

He grinned and gripped her hips. "I'm all for equal opportunity."

CHAPTER 11

THE NEXT MORNING, Cage woke before Emily and lay for a while enjoying the warmth of her body pressed against his. It was still dark outside, no light shining through the little windows. He checked his watch. As soon as it was light enough, they'd have to head down the hill.

Though it was warm in the sleeping bag with her body next to his, the air in the cabin was chilly. The fire had burned down. He didn't want to stoke it again as they would be leaving shortly.

Cage carefully slipped out of the sleeping bag without waking Emily and tucked the corners around her to keep her warm. Shivering in the cold, he dressed quickly. As good as the thought of a hot cup of coffee sounded, he'd need a fire to heat it up. All that could wait until they got back down to the lodge where, knowing Gunny, they'd have breakfast already cooked and ready for the staff and guests.

Cage had just pulled a sweatshirt over his head when he heard the squeak of the bedsprings beside him.

"Hey," Emily said, her voice hoarse from sleep. "No fair."

He chuckled. "What's not fair?"

Her brow furrowed. "You're dressed."

"You want me to get your clothes for you so you can dress inside the sleeping bag?"

"Mmm, or you could get undressed and join me."

He shook his head. "I'd love to, but you wanted to get down the mountain as soon as possible."

Emily pouted. "You had to be the voice of reason so early?"

He laughed. "I tried to get you to cancel your appointments. The offer stands. Do you want me to get your clothes for you?"

She shook her head. "No, thank you. I'll get up." She flung the sleeping bag back. Her eyes widened, and she flipped it back over her. "Holy smokes, you could have warned me it was that cold. I bet it's not even fifty degrees in here."

"That's probably a pretty close guess. Seriously, you want me to get your clothes for you?"

"No," she said and gritted her teeth. "I can do this." Once again, she tossed the sleeping bag aside and jumped out on the wood floor in her bare feet, grabbed a sweatshirt, and yanked it over her head.

Now Cage wished he would have stoked that fire, so he'd have a little bit longer to enjoy the view before Emily covered her body. He wrapped his arms around her and held her close, rubbing her back and arms to warm her skin.

Emily slipped her chilled hands beneath his sweatshirt and pressed them against his chest.

He bent to kiss her lips. "How do you feel this morning?"

She smiled up at him. "Cold, sore...and deliciously satisfied."

He grinned, smacked her ass and said, "Get dressed the rest of the way, or we won't make it down this mountain."

"Man, I'm rethinking my decision to go to work today," she said. "I'd call in sick, but I don't have reception on my cellphone."

He lifted the satellite phone from the table. "You could use this one."

"You don't even know how tempted I am." She sighed. "I can't. I need to go in to work. I need to see these guys I have scheduled to come in this week. Hopefully, one of them is the one causing us all these problems and we can put this investigation to rest."

"Are you sure you want to go in?" Cage held out the satellite phone. "All you have to do is call in sick."

She started to reach for it, and then tucked her

hand up close to her chest. "I can't. My patients need me, and one of them is likely the problem. I want to find that person. I'm tired of living in fear. And I'm tired of putting my friends and family in danger. In between sessions, I'm going to be looking in my files for any red flags that might indicate somebody who's gone off the deep end."

"Well, you know you'll have to get me past the security guards this time, because I'm not going to let you go in there alone."

She nodded. "We shouldn't have a problem. They're open for business during the weekdays."

"Well, you had your chance." He placed the satellite phone on the table and turned to her. "And just so you know what you're missing…" He slid his hands beneath her sweatshirt and smoothed them upward to cup her breasts.

She drew in a deep breath, her breasts rising as he touched the tips of her nipples. "Okay," she said breathlessly, "you made your point.

He grinned. "Yes, I have, but I'm not through." His hands slid around her back and down to cup her naked bottom. He lifted her and wrapped her legs around his waist. She settled her sex over the ridge beneath his denim fly. "Still wanna get down the mountain fast?" he asked.

She shook her head. "I can…spare a few minutes."

He laughed and laid her down on the bed, unbuckled his belt and lowered his zipper. Then he leaned over the side of the bed, fished into his shaving kit, cursed a couple of times and finally came up with a packet. He ripped it open, pulled out the condom and rolled it down his already engorged cock.

Cage laughed as Emily quicky guided him into her, setting the pace, fast and furious. She planted her heels on the mattress and met him thrust for thrust. They made the bed squeal with their exuberance. She came first, and he was right behind her, his cock throbbing inside her tight walls.

She inhaled deeply and let it out on a sigh. "You weren't kidding when you said make it quick."

"I promise I'll take my time tonight. Right now, you'd better get dressed. You can't ride down the mountain half naked."

He pulled her to her feet.

Emily dressed quickly in jeans and boots and slipped into her jacket. While she dressed, he worked with the potbelly stove to make sure the fire was tamped down enough that he felt comfortable leaving it.

The embers were still warm, but the flames had gone out. The cabin might retain some of its heat for when they returned that night. He looked forward to making his way up here again with her. If she wasn't so set on going to work, he could spend the entire day there and not worry at all about her stalker. But Emily was right. The sooner they identified the person, the sooner they could put him away.

The ride down the mountain was a little scarier than going up. On the incline, they'd leaned forward. Going down, Cage felt like he was pitching forward. Every time Emily went around a bend that he couldn't see past he worried until he could see that she was safe again. All in all, it made for a tense ride to the bottom.

The sun was just coming up over the top of the peaks when they arrived at the barn. Jake and Max emerged from inside, dusting straw off their jeans.

Emily shut down her engine and climbed off the four-wheeler. Cage did the same.

"How did it go up there?" Jake asked. "We assumed you had no problems since we didn't get any calls on the satellite phone."

"It went well," Cage said.

Emily nodded, her cheeks turning a soft pink.

Cage had to fight the urge to smile, knowing that if he did the guys would figure out pretty quickly what had happened up in the cabin. As it was, Max was looking at him with a quirk at the corners of his lips. Cage willed the man to keep his mouth shut.

"How did it go here?" Emily asked.

Jake raised his hands palms up. "Fine. Nothing happened. No new spray paint on the bar. No more flower deliveries."

Emily breathed a sigh of relief. "Good, well, I hate

to keep it short, but I'm going to get a shower and change into my work clothes. I have to go to work today." She turned to Cage. "I'll only be a few minutes, and you can have the bathroom after me."

Cage's gaze followed Emily as she headed toward the house. He trailed her at a slower pace.

"How was roughing it with no electricity?" Jake asked, as he fell in step with Cage. "It got pretty cold last night. Did you guys stay warm?"

Cage nodded; the fewer words he used the better.

Max joined them.

"RJ tells us that Gunny switched out the bunks for a single full-size mattress," Jake said.

There it was. Both Jake and Max grinned.

"So, which one of you slept on the floor?" Max asked.

"Shut the fuck up." Cage picked up the pace and left the two jokers behind.

Jake and Max's laughter followed him.

When he reached the lodge, he went directly to the kitchen. He needed that cup of coffee now, even if he had to run the gauntlet of RJ and Gunny. He was halfway through the dining room, when RJ emerged from the kitchen carrying a couple plates full of eggs, bacon and toast. "Good morning, Cage," she called out. She turned to lay the plates on the table in front of the Daughtrys. "Can I get you a refill of your coffee or orange juice?"

"We're fine," Mrs. Daughtry said. "Thank you, RJ. Go eat your breakfast."

She smiled at the older couple and turned to follow Cage into the kitchen. "Everything work out all right last night?"

"Yes, ma'am," Cage responded.

"Did you sleep well?" she persisted.

He stopped in front of the coffee pot and pulled a cup from the cabinet above, pouring some of the dark brew into the mug. He could see the smirk on RJ's face out of the corner of his eye. "I slept fine."

"On the floor?" RJ cocked an eyebrow in challenge.

Gunny set a pan on the stove a little harder than necessary. "Leave the man alone, RJ. What they did in that cabin last night is none of your business."

Cage refrained, but barely, from saying thanks. He was safe from further questioning when Swede walked through the swinging door.

"Hank's got a contact inside the Colorado Springs Metro Crime Lab. He's going to get me access to those fingerprints taken from Emily's apartment. Hopefully, they've weeded out those belonging to you and Emily. While the state police are going through the criminal records, I'll see what I can find as far as military records go."

"Good, let me know how it goes. Now, if you'll excuse me, I need to get a shower." He escaped the kitchen before RJ could start another round of questioning. He needed to warn Emily before she came down for coffee and breakfast.

He took the steps to the second floor of the lodge two at a time and arrived at the top at the same time that Emily emerged from the bathroom, wrapped in a towel. Immediately his groin tightened. She looked past him and then tipped her head toward her bedroom door. Without speaking a word, they both walked inside.

He closed the door behind them, pushed her up against the wall and claimed her mouth. The towel slipped from around her and dropped to the floor.

He growled. "You're calling in sick, right?"

She slid her calf along the back of his leg, pressing her sex against the top of his thigh and then sighed. "No, as much as I'd like to continue this, I need to get ready for work."

He smacked her naked bottom. "Tease."

She grinned. "I'm saving it for one of those next times. Tonight. In the cabin."

He kissed her again. "You're on." He left her room, ducked into his for clothes and paused when he saw his backpack.

"I haven't forgotten you, buddy. I know you'd love Emily if you were here. Wish us luck today." He grabbed the clothes he'd need and hit the shower, finishing in five minutes. He towel-dried, dressed and was out in the hall when Emily came out of her bedroom.

She blinked. "Wow, you are quick."

"I can be when I need to be."

She slid her hand in his, and they walked down the stairs together. At the bottom, she started to let go but he held on tighter. "Word of warning...everybody knows there was only one bed in that cabin. They've assumed that we made use of it."

Emily's cheeks heated. "Okay then," she said. "How about we get our breakfast to go so we don't have to suffer the inquisition."

Cage nodded. "I agree with that a hundred percent. I've already suffered the snickers."

Emily grimaced. "Is that going to hurt you where your job is concerned?"

Cage laughed. "I seriously doubt that, especially considering RJ and Jake are now together and Max and JoJo are a thing. They both set the precedent for breaking the rules."

Emily gave a firm nod and squeezed his hand, refusing to let go. "Coffee and an egg sandwich, and I'm good to go."

"Let's do it."

They marched through the great room and passed through the dining room. Emily waved at the Daughtrys as they hurried by. When they pushed though the swinging door into the kitchen, RJ, Gunny, JoJo, Max and Jake were all there, gathering platters of breakfast food to carry out to the dining room.

"Hold on just a minute," Emily said. "We want to

make up some sandwiches and a couple of mugs of coffee to go."

"Don't you have time to join us for breakfast?" Gunny asked.

Cage shook his head. "Sorry. We need to get on the road to make sure Emily's at work on time."

"You know," Emily said, her cheeks bright pink, "traffic and all."

"Yeah." RJ winked. "Avoiding us?"

"Not at all," Cage said, pasting an innocent look on his face.

"Uh huh." RJ narrowed her eyes for a long moment then sighed. "Spoil sports. Fine. I'll pour the coffee."

"And I'll make the sandwiches," Gunny offered.

Two minutes later, Cage and Emily left with their sandwiches and coffee cups, after everybody in the kitchen but Gunny graced them with devilish grins.

Once out in the rental SUV, Emily sat back in her seat. Cage slid behind the steering wheel and started the engine. "That wasn't painful in the least," Emily said. She shot a glance toward Cage and burst out laughing.

He laughed with her and realized that he'd be in deep trouble if he wasn't careful. He could very easily fall in love with this woman. As he came to think about it, it didn't sound like such a bad idea after all.

CHAPTER 12

EMILY SMILED ALL the way into Colorado Springs. Traffic was terrible, but they still managed to get to the VA hospital on time. She even had a few minutes to go through the patient file of her first appointment. Cage settled in a chair in the corner of her little office, prepared to provide her protection, should she need it, with any one of her patients. Emily smiled at his dedication and good looks. She liked having him close as she scanned her notes.

She'd been seeing Scott Chandler once a week for the past month. He had a classic case of PTSD, having been in an intense battle with mortars exploding all around him as his unit had charged a machine gun nest in Iraq. He'd left the Army after eight years of service and four deployments. He'd lost friends in battle, and his marriage was on the rocks.

He hadn't sought help for PTSD until his wife insisted as part of their marriage counseling.

Scott had a job in a manufacturing facility, working the night shift making semiconductors for computers. He'd agreed on the PTSD counseling because he didn't want his marriage to fall apart. He'd told Emily on several occasions that he loved his wife, and he wanted to keep his family together. He'd do anything to make that happen.

Surely a guy who cared that much about his wife and family wouldn't be out threatening another woman and delivering flowers to her.

Emily left her inner office and took a seat in the outer office where she conducted sessions with individual patients. This room had a couch and an armchair and muted lighting to make people feel comfortable.

Scott arrived looking better than he had in a while, and he actually smiled when he said hello.

"How's it going?" she asked.

His smile broadened. "I did like you suggested and took my wife out on a date."

"That's great. How did it go?"

"Great, but the best part was what I did before the date."

"Oh yeah?" Emily's eyes narrowed. "What was that?"

"You know how I said she's always tired when she gets home from work? Well, because it was my day off, instead of sleeping during the day, I spent time cleaning the house from top to bottom. I scrubbed the bathrooms, mopped the floors, did the dishes, all the laundry and got it folded and put away. When the kids got home from school, I had them do their homework immediately. By the time my wife got home, she had nothing left to do but get dressed and go out."

"That was a really lovely gift you gave her."

He grinned. "That's what she said. I guess I never realized how much work she did on top of a fulltime job. I promised I would help a lot more, and that we would share the responsibility of taking care of the house and the children. I can't believe she put up with me all these years. Yeah, I couldn't help her during deployments, but I should have done more when I was home."

"Scott, that's huge. I take it she was really happy?"

He nodded. "We ate at her favorite Chinese restaurant, and I took her to listen to jazz music, which normally I can't stand, and she loves. And the funny thing is…I liked it."

"I'm glad to see you being open-minded and trying new things."

"We had the best time, even better than when we were dating as teenagers." The man practically glowed over his success.

Emily's heart swelled for him. "Now that you know what it takes, what are you going to do?"

His grin broadened. "I've already started. I make sure I pick up after myself and her if I need to. I don't leave dirty dishes in the sink, and if I'm home when the kids get off the bus, I help them with their homework. I'm spending more time with my kids, and I'm taking pride in my home."

"How about the nightmares?"

He shrugged. "I still have them, but they're becoming less frequent. I'm learning to deal with them and not letting them get me down. I'm learning that when I'm down, everyone around me is down." He lifted his chin. "Life's too short to be sad all the time."

Emily nodded. "So, are you thinking you don't need me anymore?"

Scott shook his head. "Maybe, but I want to keep coming. Dr. Strayhorn, you're a good listener, and you see things I don't always see. I really am trying some of the techniques that you've given me to deal with the nightmares. And I also want my wife to know that I care enough to keep coming."

"We can move your appointments to every other week for a while and then go to once a month."

"That would be good," Scott said. "I can't thank you enough for all you've done for me and my family."

After Scott left through the doorway into the hall, Emily turned to her office on the opposite end from the session room. She'd purposely left the door opened a crack with Cage inside, ready in case one of her patients proved to be her stalker.

She slipped inside and closed the door behind her. "You really aren't supposed to be listening to my sessions. It violates HIPAA privacy standards."

"Yeah, but they can't prosecute you if you're dead. I prefer to bend a few rules than to risk your life." He tipped his chin toward the outer office.

Emily shook her head. "It couldn't be him. That man loves his wife."

"Could he have multiple personalities, and the one you saw today was the good one?" Cage waggled his eyebrows.

She shook her head. "No, I don't think so. I've never seen any indication of Dissociative Identity Disorder." She sat in her desk chair and brought up her computer screen. "My next patient will be here in fifteen minutes. I need to make notes."

"Don't mind me. I'll just sit in the corner and keep my mouth shut."

Emily grinned. She liked having him nearby. And true to his word, he didn't say anything while she made her notes in Scott's case file and brought up her next veteran on the computer.

Her next patient was a recovering alcoholic, who spent the next forty minutes whining about how nobody understood him. Emily had seen him off and on for two or three months. Nothing in his file or demeanor made her think that he might be her stalker. He was too busy moaning about his own life to disturb someone else's.

She had one other patient before lunch, a female who had suffered military sexual trauma at the hands of her first sergeant. She hadn't told anyone until she had separated from the military. And only then had she revealed what had happened and who'd done it to her for fear that he might be doing it to other women.

She'd been working with self-esteem and self-worth issues ever since and refused to be alone with a man, which Emily thoroughly understood. Like JoJo, she had taken self-defense lessons and had become so good at it she was teaching other women who had gone through the same trauma she had. Day by day, she was becoming stronger, but she still needed help and appreciated when somebody listened and gave her constructive ways to work through her issues.

At lunch, Emily took Cage to the hospital's cafeteria. "The food's not great, but it's fast and easy." After getting their food, they settled at a table in a far corner of the cafeteria. Cage had selected a hamburger and French fries, Emily a club sandwich with an apple.

"Do you have appointments all afternoon?" he asked.

"I do, unless I have a no-show, which happens more often than you'd think," she said. "If I do have a no-show, I'll use that time to look through the rest of my files. What are you doing to entertain yourself?"

"I've been texting Swede. He's still waiting on fingerprints from the crime lab. He thinks they'll be getting those right after lunch. A latent print specialist was out all morning. He's been going through some of the criminal databases tapping into guys with restraining orders on them and cross-checking to see which ones had military back-grounds and are veterans. It's a longshot but doing something is better than doing nothing."

"Has he had any hits yet?"

Cage shook his head. "It's like sifting through mud to find a specific speck of dirt."

"And I really dislike looking at all my patients as if they're the one. It's sad when one person makes it bad for everyone else. We really need to nail this guy," she said, "so we can all get on with our lives."

Cage nodded.

"Have you thought anymore about where and when you're going to release Ryan's ashes?" Emily asked.

Cage shook his head. "Not really, I've been pretty busy on this case."

"You should take your time. He obviously meant a lot to you."

"Yes, he did. He deserves a real send-off."

"A hero's send-off?" she asked.

Cage shook his head. "He was a hero, but he

wouldn't have liked anything grandiose. He didn't want the twenty-one-gun salute. He didn't want to be buried in Arlington Cemetery. He just wanted to go where the mountains were high, the air was clear and he could go back to nature. He loved the outdoors, he loved running, and he always wanted to learn to fly but never got around to it. I figured by spreading his ashes in the mountains, the wind will pick him up and carry him. He'll finally get to fly."

Emily stared across the table at Cage, falling more in love with every passing minute. It frightened and exhilarated her at the same time. What if he never returned the feeling? "Ryan was a lucky man to have you as a friend."

Cage stared out the window, his face so sad it made Emily's chest ache. "He'd have been luckier if he had lived."

"True," she whispered. "But we can't play God and determine who's going to come home and who's going to go."

Cage shook his head. "No, we can't. I'm living proof of that." Cage glanced down at his watch. "When's your next appointment?"

Emily looked at hers. "Shoot. In five minutes. We need to get going."

The rest of her afternoon went much like her morning. Once again, nothing in her patients' demeanors or in their files raised red flags. She didn't have any no-shows, so she didn't have the chance to start glancing through the rest of her patient files, which was going to take a long time anyway. After her last patient left, Emily entered her inner office. "Give me thirty minutes going through my files for tomorrow morning, and I'll be ready to go."

"Take your time," he said.

She entered her notes in her last patient's online record, and then brought up her patient load for the next day. She was tired, and her neck was stiff. Sitting up straight, she rolled her head right then left.

The chair behind her squeaked. Cage's hands descended on her shoulders and massaged the knots out. After several minutes, she leaned back against him. "You know, I can look at this tomorrow. I have a few minutes before the first guy comes in. Let's head out." If she was honest with herself, she'd own up to the excitement she felt about going back to the cabin. Instead, she told herself she was tired and ready to call it a day. Which she was, calling it a day at the office. Once they got up to the cabin, she'd have a whole different outlook.

As she left the VA hospital and walked out to the parking garage, she held her breath, afraid they'd find the rental SUV banged up like they'd found Cage's truck the day before.

The SUV was where they'd left it. Untouched. Perhaps because the parking lot was busy and people were constantly coming and going, her stalker hadn't taken his anger out on Cage's vehicle. Whatever the reason, it was nice to get in and not find a rose on the seat. Maybe because of having the police investigating and the county sheriff on the case, her stalker would back down.

That or he was waiting to catch her with her guard down.

CHAPTER 13

WHEN EMILY GASPED, Cage let his foot off the accelerator. "What? What's wrong?"

She held her hand out, her face contorted in fear. "This was in my purse."

He looked her direction briefly, "What is it?" and returned his attention to the road.

"It's a necklace with a heart-shaped pendant on it."

"Is it yours?" he asked.

She shook her head. "This is the first time I've ever seen it. And look, it has the initials JR on it. But it's what's on the other side that scares me."

Cage frowned, his pulse kicking up. "What's on the other side?" He shot another quick glance in her direction.

Emily swallowed hard, her eyes filling with tears.

"Do I need to pull over?" Cage asked. Not that

they could. They were in the middle of the pass. There was no place to pull over.

She shook her head. "The inscription says, *I will have you*."

Cage's brow furrowed. "Like the poem?"

Emily stared down at the pendant and spoke softly. "Roses are red. Violets are blue. Sugar is sweet. And *I will have you*."

Cage's gut clenched. "How'd he get to your purse? I was in there the whole time."

Emily shook her head. "No, you weren't. We both left for lunch, and I didn't take my purse. Just my wallet."

"But you locked the door to your office."

She laughed. "That doesn't seem to matter to this guy. Locks aren't even a challenge. He put this in my purse today."

"Are you sure it wasn't in there before?"

She shook her head. "No, I looked in that pocket this morning for my lip balm. The necklace wasn't there. He had to have done it during lunch."

"And you say it had initials on the other side—JR?"

She nodded. "Yes."

"This could be the breakthrough we've needed. If those are his initials that narrows down our list of potential suspects considerably. Do we need to go back to your office? I can turn around."

She laughed. "No, you can't. We're in the pass. We

can't turn around until we get to the other end. No," she said, "let's just go on to the lodge. Besides, if we went back to my office, and I spent a couple hours looking online, we wouldn't get back to the lodge in time to go up to the cabin. With the stalker still actively pursuing me, I couldn't stay at the lodge."

Cage nodded. "And you can't stay at your apartment."

"Obviously not. Locks mean nothing to him. Besides, I've got a list of names I downloaded onto a flash drive. I can sort them by J and R and I could use those names to tap into the database that Swede is going to hook me up with."

Cage increased their speed as they emerged from the winding roads of the pass. "Those databases would be better use of our time, anyway."

Emily shook her head. "Not your time…mine. I have to be the one looking for the names."

He nodded. "Of course, but Swede can be around to answer any questions."

"And I'm sure I'll have them." Emily dropped the necklace in the cupholder as if it was burning her fingers.

Cage would have Swede look at it to see if he could figure out where it might have come from and who might have engraved it. The letters weren't just scratched on. They were professionally engraved.

He drove through the town of Fool's Gold and out the highway toward Lost Valley Ranch. He was reassured to see that the bar still had a clean coat of paint on it and there were no sheriff's vehicles outside.

Horses grazed in the pasture and a couple of the lodge's guests were sitting on the front porch. At least at Lost Valley Ranch, everything was back to normal.

Cage parked in front of the lodge, got out and came around to help Emily down.

She reached into the cupholder for the necklace and handed it to him. "Here, I don't want it."

He nodded and slipped it into his pocket to give to Swede later. They walked up the steps hand in hand and entered the lodge.

RJ called out from the dining area. "Oh, good, you're here. We were just about to serve supper."

Emily shook her head. "I'm not hungry."

Cage touched a hand to the small of her back. "You need to eat. There's some food up at the cabin, but nothing like what you can get here that Gunny has fixed for you."

RJ frowned and crossed the great room, closing the distance between her and Emily. "What's wrong? Did he show up at your office?"

"He did," Emily said.

RJ's eyes widened. "Who was it?"

Emily's lips pressed together. "I don't know. He broke into my locked office and dropped a necklace in my purse."

"How the hell is he getting into all these locked offices, buildings and cars?" RJ shook her head. "Show me."

Cage pulled the necklace out of his pocket and handed it to RJ. "We really should be protecting it from fingerprints, but I figure as small as it is, whatever prints might have been there are already smudged."

"JR?" RJ laughed. "Those are my initials transposed." She flipped it over. "*I will have you.*"

"It's the rhyme," Emily said.

"Oh yeah. Roses are red. Violets are blue. Sugar is sweet, and I will have you. That's not how it goes."

"That's how he wants it to go," Emily said. "I don't think he plans on taking no for an answer."

"He's not going to get the chance to get to you," Cage said. He would make sure of it.

"Well, the guy's obviously an idiot." RJ held the necklace out. "He left his initials on it."

Cage pocketed the necklace.

"Come eat dinner," RJ said. "You're going to need your strength. Swede said he's got everything set up for you as soon as you're done eating."

"I'm not—" Emily started.

RJ held up a hand. "You *will* eat supper. You can't let this guy rule your life. You only have a couple short hours before it gets too dark to make it up to the cabin. So, stop arguing and get to the dining table now."

Emily smiled. "Yes, ma'am."

Cage guided Emily to the dining table with a hand the small of her back.

JoJo and Max helped Gunny carry the food out to the lodge guests first, and then everyone went back into the kitchen to carry out the platters for the staff's table.

Gunny brought out a platter of chicken cordon bleu and set it in the middle of the table. "Emily, I made your favorite. I hope you're hungry."

She gave him a weak smile and said, "It smells really good."

"And I made fresh rolls as well." He pulled aside a dish towel over a bowl filled with giant bread rolls. The scent filled the room.

Though his stomach was knotted, Cage's mouth watered.

To go with the main course, Gunny had also made roasted asparagus and a garden salad.

Swede arrived at the table, and they all took their seats.

Cage passed the necklace around and explained what had happened as the lodge staff and the Brotherhood Protectors filled their plates.

"Hopefully, he's backed off destroying property," Jake said.

"But he's still giving her gifts," JoJo commented. "Which means, he hasn't given up yet."

"I feel like we're playing a game of cat and mouse,"

Emily said. "What does he expect? When will h
make an appearance? Why doesn't he get it over
with?" She sighed.

"I'm just afraid of how he'll show up," RJ said.
"This sneaking around crap has us all nervous. And
the damage he did to Cage's truck demonstrates a
violent streak. You need to make sure Cage is with
you at all times."

"Believe me," Emily said. "I will. Until we catch
this guy, Cage and I will be joined at the hip."

"I'm glad you two are staying at the cabin," RJ
said. "It's remote enough to keep your stalker
guessing as to where you are. But to make sure you're
not being followed, I think Jake and I will escort you
halfway up the trail."

Cage nodded. "I'd appreciate that." Having
another set of eyes on the trail would make him feel
better about being so isolated.

The chicken cordon bleu was delicious. Cage ate
every bite and a couple of the dinner rolls. His time
in the Army had taught him to eat when he could
because he might not get to later. A soldier had to
provide fuel for his body so that he had sufficient
energy to face the enemy.

Emily, on the other hand, picked at her food,
staring at the necklace lying between her and Cage
on the table.

He picked it up and handed it to Swede. "See if

you can trace this to where it was purchased or engraved."

Swede grimaced. "I'll do the best I can but don't expect miracles. I'm really hoping that Emily will find something on the databases, now that you have some initials to go by." He pushed back in his seat. "I'm finished, Emily. If you're ready, I'll get you started."

She perked up and scooted back in her chair. "Let's do this." She stood and collected her plate, ready to carry it into the kitchen.

"Leave it," JoJo said. "Max and I will clean up. You go."

Swede led the way into the basement. Emily followed and Cage brought up the rear. Swede went straight to the bank of computer monitors, pulled out the keyboard tray and tapped on the keys. A couple of the monitors blinked to life.

Emily handed him the flash drive.

He plugged it in and scanned it for viruses. When it was cleared, he showed her where to access it. "And by the way," he said, "the latent print expert said they did not find any other fingerprints besides yours and Cage's among those prints they lifted. Your stalker had to have been wearing gloves when he entered your apartment."

Cage's lips pressed firmly together. Nothing about this investigation was going to be easy. He hoped that the databases Swede was tapping into would do the trick and lead them to their guy.

"Once you get your names sorted by the initials, run those names against the criminal database." He showed her how to perform a search and narrow it down by location. He brought her up on another database using a different monitor. "You can toggle back and forth between these two." He showed her how. "This database contains information about military personnel. Start by sorting. Narrow it down to inactive, for now, and an address here in Colorado. If he's one of your patients, he should have a local address."

She nodded.

"If you need any more help, just yell. I'll be here, but I promise not to look over your shoulder."

"Thanks, Swede." She glanced across the room at Cage.

He smiled. "Go for it, and don't mind me. I can play solitaire on my phone."

She got to work.

Cage studied her while she wasn't looking his direction. She wasn't beautiful in the photogenic, movie-star kind of way. Still, she was pretty, with her auburn hair curling around her face and down to her shoulders. He loved the way her green eyes sparkled when she got excited about something, and her smile made him warm all over.

Emily was the kind of person that, if he was in a

crowded room, she'd be the one that he'd be looking for. And when he'd found her, he'd feel complete.

Cage wondered what Ryan would have thought of her. They'd discussed the kind of women they thought they wanted to marry. Emily wasn't anything like what he'd pictured in a wife. He'd thought he'd have gone for a blonde with blue eyes. Now that he knew Emily, he realized there was more to the color of her hair and her eyes. The real beauty of a person was what was inside. And Emily was beautiful all the way through.

An hour and a half into her search Emily sighed, stood and stretched. "It's getting late. I've done enough for today."

Cage leaped to his feet. "Did you find any potential suspects?"

Her lips pressed together. "Maybe."

"On the criminal database? Or on the military one?" Swede asked.

She pressed her lips together. "Both."

Feeling the first spark of hope in the past couple of days, Cage grinned. "That's promising."

Emily gave him a twisted smile. "I don't want to get my hopes up. I didn't make it through all the J and R names."

"What kind of crimes did you find on your guys on the criminal database?" Swede asked.

"One of them was caught selling drugs," she said.

"He got probation. Another had a restraining order against him to stay away from his ex-wife."

"Any more?" Cage asked.

Emily shook her head. "Not so far. I got about halfway through my list of patients with a J and an R initial. I have to continue tomorrow."

"Any chance those two have appointments in your office this week?"

Her face grim, Emily nodded. "I have one of them in an individual appointment tomorrow, and the other in a group appointment on Wednesday."

"You need to cancel that individual appointment," Cage said.

Emily shook her head. "No way. If he's the one, I want him to show himself. Besides, I'll have you close by."

"Close might not be good enough," Cage said. "Is tomorrow the drug dealer or the restraining order?"

"Restraining order."

"You're definitely cancelling that appointment." Cage frowned. He didn't like Emily putting herself out there with a man who'd shown a tendency toward violence. "Do you think we can get a court order to have him and his apartment searched?"

Swede shook his head. "At this point, I don't think we have enough evidence. Plus, we'd be answering questions about how we obtained our information."

"And I really don't want to single out anyone who might not be the stalker." Emily shook her head.

"These guys have enough strikes against them. That could set them back on any kind of strides they've made in improving their mental health."

Cage clenched his fists. "I don't like it."

"You think I do?" Emily asked.

"At the very least," he said, "I'm going with you to the group session."

She nodded. "I think we could finagle that. We just have to get through tomorrow."

"Are any of your other individual appointments tomorrow with anybody with a J or an R in their name?" Cage asked.

"I don't think so." Emily's eyes narrowed. "But I can't remember all of them." She pulled her flash drive from the computer and slipped it into her pocket. "Right now, we need to get up the mountain. I don't want to be trail riding in the dark. And I won't stay here and put everybody at risk. I need to change into something I can wear on the four-wheeler, and I'll be ready."

"Me, too," Cage said.

"I'll let RJ and Jake know to have the four-wheelers out and ready to go," Swede said.

"Thank you, Swede," Emily said. "For everything."

The big guy nodded. "We'll hit it again tomorrow."

Cage followed Emily up the stairs. After she entered her room and closed the door, he went to his room, changed into some old jeans and a T-shirt. He slipped his handgun into a shoulder holster, shrugged into a warm jacket and came back out into the hallway.

Emily wasn't far behind. As she came out of her room, she was slipping a 38-caliber pistol into a shoulder holster, and she carried a jacket in her other hand.

"Ready?"

She nodded.

RJ and Jake were waiting outside the barn with four ATVs, their engines running. The noise from the engines prevented the exchange of words.

Emily mounted her four-wheeler and headed for the gate.

Cage slipped in behind her.

Max and JoJo were at the gate with it opened wide. As soon as the four ATVs were through, Max closed the gate.

The only time Emily slowed on the ride up the mountain was around corners or when the trail became too rocky.

Halfway to the cabin, RJ and Jake peeled off, leaving Cage and Emily to complete the journey on their own.

They arrived at the cabin fifteen minutes later.

Emily stood back and let Cage be first through the door. He found the flashlight on the wall and shined it quickly around the interior, looking for anything different, small or large. Everything looked the same as when they'd left that morning. He opened the door wide and Emily walked in.

"I'll start the generator," he said.

Emily nodded. "I'll bring in some logs."

Before long, they had a fire burning in the potbelly stove, warming the interior of the little cabin quickly.

"I'm going to get my shower," she said with a tight smile. "I won't be long."

He poured water from one of the water bottles into a pan and placed it on the stove to warm. While Emily was in the shower, he took the two mugs they'd used the night before out to the stream and rinsed them clean. He was back before it got too dark to see. He closed the door and moved the latch in place. It wasn't a lock that somebody could pick. It was a heavy wooden latch. To get in, someone would have to use a pretty hefty battering ram to break down the door.

Hopefully, he didn't have to worry about that. They were far enough up in the mountains that Emily's stalker shouldn't be able to find them. Then again, the bastard had proven himself resourceful.

Cage laid his handgun on the table where he could reach it quickly, stripped out of his jacket and the shoulder holster and stood with his hands held out to the potbelly stove, warming them.

A moment later, Emily appeared in the doorway to the tiny bathroom. She wore the long T-shirt, and her face was scrubbed clean of any makeup she'd worn that day. She padded barefooted across the floor, carrying her clothes, jacket and shoulder holster. She laid her things on the table, pulled her .38 out of the holster and laid it next to his 9 mm.

Then she turned to the potbelly stove and held her hands out to the heat.

"My turn," he said. "I'll only be a couple minutes."

Emily snorted. "Any longer than that, and you'll be an icicle."

With a smile, Cage ducked into the bathroom, stripped and rinsed off quickly before his skin could turn blue. When he came back out, he only had the towel to wrap around him as he'd left his shorts on the bed. He tossed his clothes on a chair.

Before he could take two more steps, Emily was in his arms, pressing her cheek against his naked chest. She didn't say anything, and he didn't feel a need to speak either. It was enough to just hold her.

When she finally raised her head, he bent to kiss her then he scooped her up in his arms and carried her to the bed. He laid her on the sleeping bag then crawled inside it with her, tugged the towel free and dropped it on the floor. Then he pulled her close so that they could share each other's body heat.

As much as he wanted to make love to her, he figured that wasn't what she needed at the moment. She needed somebody to hold her and keep the darkness away. He held her for a long time and thought she might have fallen asleep, when she stirred against him.

"Are you asleep?" she whispered.

He chuckled. "No. I thought you were."

"You want to sleep?" she asked.

"Actually, I'm wide awake." He was more than wide awake; he was aroused. All she had to do was shift her hand from his chest and slide it lower, and she'd discover that for herself.

She slid her calf over his, and her hand shifted from his chest down his torso.

Cage's breath caught and held. He wasn't going to assume anything until…

Her hands slipped lower and circled his cock.

"Are you sure you're up to this?" he asked.

"I am," she said. "And apparently, so are you."

They made love slowly, taking the time to find out what each of them liked.

After an incredibly satisfying climax, they lay for a while in each other's arms staring up at the dark ceiling.

"Are you going to sleep now, or would you like some cocoa?" he asked.

"Cocoa, please."

Cage slipped out of the warmth of the sleeping bag, pulled on his shorts and walked across the cold wooden floor to the potbelly stove. The water he'd put on to warm was hot enough now for the chocolate. He poured it into the mugs, added in the packets of cocoa mix and stirred.

Emily had pulled her shirt over her head and sat cross-legged on the bed.

He handed her the cup and slipped into the sleeping bag with her, glad for the warmth.

She sipped her cocoa quietly for a few minutes, then looked over the rim of her cup at him. "Do you think what we have here is just a short-term infatuation?"

He laughed. "You're the psychologist. You tell me."

She shook her head. "I really don't have a clue. I've never been in love." Her brow furrowed. "Is it even possible to fall in love in just a couple days?"

Cage shrugged. "You're talking to a self-professed, confirmed bachelor who's afraid of commitment because of the disappointment of childhood. My buddy Ryan and I talked about getting married and having kids, but mostly we looked at it as something of a rite of passage. We really didn't discuss falling in love." He set his empty mug of cocoa on the table beside the bed.

She handed him hers, and he set it beside his. Then he took her in his arms, and they lay back against the pillow.

"Well, what do you think now?" Emily said.

"I think we were missing the whole point of marriage and children."

She chuckled. "And what point is that?"

"Finding a partner for life. Finding someone who completes you."

"And when did you come across this discovery?" Emily asked.

He pulled her even closer. "When I met you." Then he kissed her and held her even longer. It wasn't about having sex. It was about being with someone you cared about and who cared about you.

CHAPTER 14

SURPRISINGLY, Emily had had the best night's sleep she'd had in a long time. She attributed it, not to the lumpy mattress or hot cocoa, but to the man who'd held her in his arms throughout the night.

That morning, they went through the same routine as the previous day, making love quickly before saddling up on the ATVs for the early morning ride down to the lodge. Emily showered, changed into nice work clothes, grabbed breakfast sandwiches and coffee to go, and headed out.

Jake and RJ offered to go with them to the VA hospital as backup. However, there was no sense in having so many people sitting around her office.

If she ran into any difficulties, Cage would be there, and they could call the hospital police. As it was, they couldn't take their weapons on campus.

Hopefully, neither could her stalker. No guns or knives were allowed inside government facilities.

Emily prepared for her day like any other day, by going through her patient files before each appointment to remind herself of that person's issues and progress. She tried to focus on each patient and his needs, when all she could think about was the one veteran she'd confront that afternoon.

Jason Romig.

The criminal database had him listed as having a restraining order his ex-wife had filed against him, claiming he was abusive. Emily had seen Jason on a number of occasions but had never seen that violent streak in him. Then again, some of the so-called nicest people turned out to be serial killers.

After each session, Emily retreated to her inner office, where Cage would rub the knots out of her shoulders and ask her how she was holding up. She lied each time, telling him she was fine when her insides were wound up tighter than a top. The man had to see through her lie based on the tension he could feel in her muscles.

She barely ate a bite of her salad at lunch. By the time her one o'clock appointment with Jason Romig rolled around, she was nervous. She could barely focus on her computer monitor as she prepared for the session.

"Let me go in with you," Cage said.

Emily shook her head. "You can't. And you really

aren't supposed to be in here," she said, glancing around her inner office.

"I'm not leaving you alone with him."

"Then just listen through the crack in the door," Emily advised.

"I don't feel good about this," Cage said. "But I know you're going to do this no matter what I say. Don't hesitate to cry out for help if you feel at all threatened."

She nodded. "I will."

Emily stepped into the room where the session would take place and closed the door to her inner office, leaving a gap of five inches. She sat in the armchair, leaving the couch open for Jason. Then, with her heart pounding against her ribs, she waited for her patient to arrive.

Five minutes after the scheduled appointment time, Emily's hands were sweating, and she was ready to bolt.

Jason Romig walked into the room. The man was bigger than she remembered from the last time he'd been in her office. His broad shoulders seemed to fill the room, and he was a little on the heavy side. He looked like he could snap her like a twig.

He came in with a snarl on his face and dropped onto the couch.

"Good afternoon, Jason." She had to force a natural, soothing tone to her voice, when in fact she was terrified. The only thing that kept her calm was the knowledge that Cage was in the other room, a few short feet away from her.

"How have you been over the past week, Jason?" Emily asked.

"Great...just great," he said, sarcasm dripping from his tone.

"You don't sound great," Emily said. "Is something wrong?"

"I got a goddammed ticket as I was driving in today. I was only going five miles per hour over the effing speed limit. It wasn't like I was driving reck-lessly." Jason snorted. "Idiot cop."

"I'm sorry to hear that." Emily took a steadying breath and plunged in. "Is there anything else both-ering you that you'd like to talk about during this session?"

He looked up. "As a matter of fact, there is." He leaned forward, resting his elbows on his knees. "I really need to get past this PTSD bullshit."

Emily forced a light laugh. "Well, that is why you're here."

"Yeah, well it's kind of ruining my life."

"Do you want to explain that to me?" she prompted.

"You know I have the nightmares, I jump at loud noises and I'm angry all the time. My wife ditched me because she couldn't handle it and, since our divorce, I've been trying to move on with my life. Now, I'm interested in a girl, and she just looks through me as if I'm not even there."

Emily tensed. "Maybe she doesn't know how you feel."

"She has to know how I feel," he said.

Emily clutched her hands together in her lap to keep them from shaking. "How does she know?"

"I've dropped hints all over the place, like giving her flowers and other gifts."

"Flowers and gifts might not be enough. Have you tried talking to her?"

Jason shrugged and looked away. "Not actually."

"Really?"

He sighed. "I'm kind of a big guy. My size sometimes intimidates women. They think just because I'm big, I'm mean."

Emily found herself nodding. She was intimidated by the man's bulk. "It's true. Women can be intimidated by a man's size. You have to remember that women are more vulnerable. They aren't always as strong as the men they might consider going out with or even the men they pass on the street. They have to be careful and not get themselves in a situation where they can be easily overpowered by a man who is much stronger and larger than them."

"Yeah," Jason said. "I get that. Men can be bastards and beat up women, but I'd never hurt this girl. She's the nicest girl I've ever known. She's really pretty and nothing like my ex-wife."

"What do you mean?" Emily asked.

"She's kind, she's honest and she would never do anything to hurt others."

Emily narrowed her eyes. "And your ex-wife wasn't kind and honest?"

"Hell, no," Jason said. "She lied to the police, telling them I abused her, when she actually beat up on me. She had me slapped with a restraining order. I couldn't even get into my own house. All I wanted was my own shit. I told her she could have all the furniture, she could have the car, she could have the goddamn house. I just wanted my clothes and the coin collection my father left me. She even got all that. I had to start all over with my clothes, and she put my father's coin collection up on eBay and sold it. She almost made me give up on women...until I met this girl." His face softened. "Do you want to see a picture of her?"

Emily sucked in a breath. In her gut, she couldn't believe that the girl he was talking about was her. She nodded. "Yes, I would like to see it."

He pulled his cellphone out of his back pocket, thumbed through his photographs, brought one up and leaned across to show her.

Emily let go of the breath she'd been holding when she saw the photograph of the young woman in the picture. She had sandy-blond hair and blue eyes. "If she doesn't know you exist, how do you have a photograph of her?"

His cheeks reddened. "I pulled it down off of her Facebook page." He cringed. "Does that make me creepy?"

"Maybe a little. You really should talk to her. Make sure it's in a neutral environment that doesn't frighten her. Because like you said, you *are* big. That could be scary to someone. You can ask her on a date, but I'd start with asking her out for coffee or a donut or something. That way she doesn't have to commit to a whole dinner date. Just ask her out like a friend." She laughed. "I'm supposed to be helping you out with your PTSD, not your love life."

"Yeah, but Doc, you're the only person I can talk to. You don't know how much I appreciate it."

"Jason, just do yourself a favor. If she's not interested in you, don't pursue her. You'll come off more like a stalker, and that won't win anyone over."

He raised his hands. "Oh, I wouldn't do that. If someone doesn't like me, I'd be wasting their time as well as mine." He looked down at the picture on his cellphone. "But I sure would like to take her out." He looked up at Emily. "Do you think I have a chance?"

"You never know until you ask, but be upfront about it. Secret admirers can be creepy."

He frowned. "You know, I never thought about that." He straightened. "Thank you, Dr. Strayhorn."

She laughed. "You have another thirty minutes on this session. Don't you want to stay and talk about your PTSD?"

"We can next time. Right now, I just want to go ask her out for some coffee. Life's too short to miss an opportunity to be happy."

"That's a healthy way to think. Good luck, Jason."

"Thank you, Dr. Strayhorn." Jason left the session room, ending Emily's day early.

As soon as the outer door closed, the inner one opened.

Cage stepped through and pulled her into his arms. "I like the way that guy thinks. Life is too short not to do the things that make you happy." He claimed her mouth in a kiss that left her completely breathless. When he came up for air he chuckled. "I take it the picture he showed you wasn't yours?"

"I have to tell you, I almost didn't want to look. Had it been me, I think I might have lost it."

"He could have been playing you, showing you a picture of some girl he didn't even know."

Emily shook her head. "No. He appeared to be on the up and up. I don't think he's our guy. We still have Jimmy Rhodes in the group session tomorrow, and I'll spend some more time looking through my list when we get to the lodge."

"I'll feel better when I can sit in the same room with you and your potential stalker."

"We can make that happen tomorrow," Emily said. "The good thing is, it's not at the end of the day. It's my group meeting right after lunch."

They left the hospital, climbed into the rented SUV and headed for Lost Valley Ranch.

Emily hadn't received any more gifts in her purse, in her office or on the seat of the car. The one person she had an appointment with that day, who could possibly have been the stalker based on his initials and his police record, didn't appear to be their guy. She almost wished it would have been. At least then, the search would have been over, and she wouldn't have another night of worry to live through.

On the other hand, whenever they caught the stalker, that would end her need for a bodyguard and their need to stay in the cabin in the mountains. If, during their group session tomorrow, Jimmy Rhodes ended up being the stalker, all the drama would come to an end. She hoped that didn't mean that her relationship with Cage would also come to an end.

CAGE WAS glad the day had ended on a high note and that Emily had not been harmed. They arrived back at the ranch early enough that Gunny had just started cooking dinner. The guys were out at the barn taking care of animals. RJ and JoJo were cleaning rooms in the lodge, preparing them for the guests to arrive the following evening.

Emily opted to change out of her work clothes into more casual clothes that she could wear riding up the mountain on an ATV. She came out of her bedroom in jeans and a sweatshirt with her hair pulled back in a ponytail. She looked more like a teenager than a highly educated psychologist.

Cage held out his hand. She slipped hers into his palm, and they walked downstairs together.

"Let's see if they need any help getting supper ready," she said.

Cage nodded and walked with her to the kitchen.

Gunny had a huge pot of chili on the stove. The scent of hamburger and onions filled the air. He was mixing cornbread batter in a large bowl when they walked in the door. He poured out the batter into a greased, cast-iron skillet.

"Whatcha making, Gunny?" Emily asked.

"Chili and cornbread for dinner," he said. "Something easy and hearty."

"Smells good," she said. "Can we help?"

He shook his head. "Got it all ready. Just has to cook for a while."

"In that case," Emily said, "I think I'll go downstairs and get to work on hunting down my stalker."

Gunny shook his head. "So, you didn't get him today, huh?"

She gave him a crooked smile. "No, not today."

"Well, maybe tomorrow."

Swede was in the basement when Emily and Cage came down the stairs. It only took him a minute to bring up the databases that Emily needed. She plugged in her flash drive and went to work identifying potential candidates.

While she worked, Cage brought Swede up to date on what had occurred during the day.

"I really hope your stalker reveals himself tomorrow," Swede said. "Hank and the others are all flying in Thursday night. I'd rather the case be resolved before they arrive."

"You and me both," Cage said. "I'll be sitting in on the session tomorrow. If her stalker is in that group, and he recognizes me, it might set him off."

"At least you'll be there if he loses his shit," Swede said.

At dinner, Emily picked at her food again. She assured Gunny that it tasted great, but she wasn't hungry. Afterward, she and Cage helped with the dishes. Then Emily claimed she was tired, and they were going to head up to the miner's cabin early.

JoJo and Max provided their escort to the halfway point, and they went on from there. They spent the first part of the night making love and then holding each other. Cage could tell the stress was getting to Emily, and he wished he could solve the case for her. He hoped the next day would prove to be the last for the stalker, and that he would be caught and sent to jail.

Catching the stalker would bring such a sense of relief. At the same time, it would leave him wondering where he would go from there. Jake would find him an assignment, and Emily might possibly move back to her apartment.

Cage stared up at the rafters in the cabin, realizing he'd miss this little place where it was drafty and cold and smelled of wood smoke. Being alone with Emily in the cabin made him want to be with her every night and wake up with her every morning. Was it possible to fall in love with somebody in just a few short days? If it was, he was well on his way.

CHAPTER 15

ON WEDNESDAY MORNING, Emily was up first. She was already dressed when Cage rolled out of bed and slipped into his jeans.

"How'd you sleep?" he asked.

She shook her head. "I didn't. I kept thinking that this could be the day we'll find out who the stalker is. The searches on Swede's databases didn't reveal any other finds. If Jimmy Rhodes isn't our guy, I don't know who is. That's the only other JR that matched both the criminal database and the military database.

Cage pulled his sweatshirt over his head and then stepped up to Emily, pulling her into his arms. "Are you sure you're up to this today?" he asked as he held her close.

She wrapped her arms around his waist and pressed her cheek to his chest. "You'll be with me. I'll be fine," she said. "It's just all the stress of not knowing and waiting. I feel like I'm holding a bomb, and I don't know when it's going to go off."

"You kind of are holding a ticking timebomb. This guy is unstable. If it comes time for the session, and you decide you don't want to do it, don't."

She shook her head. "I can't live like this, wondering every day if this will be the day he comes after me. We have to find him, preferably before the grand opening when everybody will be here."

He kissed the top of her head then tipped her chin up and claimed her lips. When he brought his head up again, he stared down into her eyes. "Are you ready?"

She shook her head. "No, but I guess we'd better go."

Like they had the previous two days, they descended the trail to the lodge, showered, changed, grabbed their food and left. Emily sat silently in the passenger seat all the way into Colorado Springs.

This could be the day. Having Cage in the therapy session could be the trigger that would set the stalker off. She hoped that nobody else in the session would be harmed and that Cage would be able to subdue the man quickly if he tried anything.

As the hour approached, she skipped lunch and paced her office, waiting for the one o'clock session to take place in the large conference room, instead of her individual session room.

Ten minutes before one, she glanced across at

Cage. "Let's do this," she said, and led the way through the building to the conference room where she arranged chairs in a semi-circle, moving the tables out of the way.

One by one, her patients arrived and took seats. Some talked with others, and others sat quietly waiting for the session to begin.

Reggie Smith took a seat next to Milo Tate, and they talked softly to each other. A couple others walked in.

Emily ticked them off on her list of names. She was watching for Jimmy Rhodes when Jay Slater walked in, and she remembered he liked to be called JR. She hadn't even looked him up on the crime or the military database because his initials weren't JR; they were JS.

He sat in the center of the semi-circle and stared straight at her, which wasn't uncommon, considering all of them looked to her to guide the session. The last two in the door were Nathan Small and Jimmy Rhodes.

Cage had slipped in halfway through the influx of people and claimed one of the seats. Jimmy's eyes narrowed when he noticed the new guy in the room. But he didn't say anything, instead taking his seat on the left edge of the group, placing him closer than the others to Emily.

She studied him in her peripheral vision. Was it her imagination or were his eyes bloodshot? And were the dark circles under his eyes more pronounced? When he sat in his chair, he rocked slightly back and forth as if nervous or strung out. His criminal record had tagged him with selling drugs. A lot of pushers did drugs themselves. His medical record had also indicated that he had done drugs in the past. For most of the group sessions, he had appeared to have kicked his habit, but today it didn't seem so. But did a bad habit make him a stalker?

She glanced from Jimmy Rhodes to JR Slater, and then her gaze slipped around to where Cage sat quietly observing those around him. Normally, this group session went well, with each person sharing his thoughts with a little prompting from Emily.

But in this particular session, the men were leaning forward. JR's leg bounced nervously. Milo drummed his fingers on his knee. And the usually good-natured Nathan stared at the floor, frowning. Maybe they sensed her tension and were reacting to it.

With two men in the group who could potentially be the stalker, Emily struggled with some method to bring him out. If he'd been watching her, he knew that Cage was the man she had been with for the last few days. Surely seeing him in the group would anger him. If she made him jealous by showing favoritism toward Cage, it might trigger him to reveal himself.

Emily drew in a deep breath, smiled directly at

Cage and tucked a strand of her hair behind her ear. Then she looked from right to left at each person in the group and asked, "How was your week?" She waited for anyone to respond, knowing they wouldn't. After three long seconds, she turned to Milo. "Milo, did you get the new tires on your vehicle?"

Milo nodded. "I did, and I nearly had a heart attack at the tire shop when they let the air pressure out of the tire. It made such a loud noise, I thought I had incoming artillery. I dropped to the ground and made an idiot of myself in front of the guys fixing the tires."

Emily shook her head. "Don't feel bad about that. If they were prior military, they'd totally understand."

Milo's lips pressed together. "They were a couple of kids, probably still in high school."

"Then they wouldn't understand, and they won't until they join the military. Loud noises are going to bother you for a while. Don't worry about what other people think."

Milo snorted. "That's easy to say but not easy to do."

Emily looked around the room for the next person to call on. She pulled in a breath and decided to jump in with both feet. She turned to JR Slater. She captured his gaze. "JR, how was your week?"

Cage looked toward JR, frowning.

JR shrugged. "It was okay, I guess," he said. "I got a job."

"That's good. What kind of job?"

"I've been working lots of hours at a bowling alley. They've been paying me overtime, so I haven't had time to practice those meditation techniques. I haven't been home much, but when I am, I just fall straight into bed. I'm exhausted."

"Good for you, getting a job." If the man was working a lot of overtime, he didn't have time to leave her gifts and bash in windows.

She turned to Jimmy Rhodes. "What about you, Jimmy?"

His head jerked around, and he looked at her as if he just realized she was in the same room. His slight rocking motion became more pronounced. "What?"

"I asked how your week went," she repeated.

"It sucked, like every week has sucked since I got out of the military. Good for JR getting a job," he said in a condescending tone. "Every time I get a job, I get laid off within a week. Your meditation techniques don't pay the bills. My unemployment ran out last month. I'm sick and tired of everything. I'm sick and tired of coming to these sessions." He lurched to his feet. "If I'm sitting here, I'm not making money. If I'm not making money, I can't afford the shit I need."

He staggered toward Emily. "The only one getting paid in this room is the pretty doctor. Maybe that's what I need. I just need to find a pretty doctor to support me. That's it, that's what I want. I want you, Dr. Strayhorn."

Cage was out of his seat and halfway across the space when Jimmy Rhodes lunged for Emily. She didn't move fast enough to get out of his way. He grabbed her and spun her around, locking his arm around her neck in a chokehold that cut off her breathing. She clutched at the arm around her neck, scratching and clawing, trying to remove it.

Cage charged toward Jimmy. "Let her go," he said.

"Don't come any closer, or I'll snap her neck." Jimmy swayed as if he was having trouble standing on his own feet.

Emily couldn't breathe. She knew the longer she didn't get air into her lungs, the sooner she would pass out. She quickly thought through the self-defense lessons she'd taken. She suddenly went limp, making her body a dead weight to her captor. Then she slumped, letting gravity drag her down and taking Jimmy with her.

He struggled to remain on his feet.

When he hunched over, Emily came up quickly, knocking her head into his chin.

He cried out, and his arm loosened around her neck enough for Emily to grab a gulp of breath and jam her elbow into his gut.

Jimmy doubled over, cursing Emily.

She broke away from him and stood breathing hard.

Cage stepped in, grabbed the man's arm and pulled it up behind his back.

Jimmy yelped. "Hey, leave me alone. I didn't mean to hurt her."

"Well, you did," Cage said. "Now you'll have to take it up with the police."

Emily's hands shook as she pulled her cellphone out of her pocket and dialed campus security. Two VA police officers appeared shortly after. They ended up calling the Colorado Springs Police Department.

Once again, the detective that had been investigating the other incidents arrived on the scene to question Jimmy. All the other patients had to remain in the room until the police got statements from them.

Once the police took custody of Jimmy, Cage crossed to Emily and took her into his arms. "Are you okay?"

She was shaking like a leaf, but she nodded. "I'm okay."

Soon, the room cleared. The detective walked Jimmy out with the help of another city police officer. As the detective left the conference room, he turned to Emily. "Ma'am, if you'll stay here, I'll be back in a few minutes."

She nodded. "I'll be here."

Emily stepped out of Cage's arms and paced the room. Time dragged. When she stuck her head out in the hall to see if the detective was on his way back, she found Nathan Small standing there. "Nathan, what are you still doing here?"

"I was worried about you. I wanted to make sure that you were okay."

"I'm fine, but you should go home."

"Well, now that I know you're okay, I will."

"Thank you for caring, Nathan."

He nodded and walked down the hall, disappearing around a corner. The detective appeared at that moment and came to sit in the conference room with her and Cage.

"What do you think, Detective?" Emily asked. "Is it him?"

The detective pulled an evidence bag out of his pocket and laid it on the table. It was a clear plastic bag, and inside it was a scrap of fabric.

Emily leaned closer and gasped. "Those are my panties." She looked up at the detective. "Where did you find those?"

His face grim, he said, "We found them in the backseat of Jimmy's car along with a bat with fingerprints all over it. We'll have to run them through the database, but we suspect that's the bat he used to destroy Mr. Weaver's truck."

Relief washed over Emily. They'd caught the guy. "Thank the lord," she said.

The detective nodded.

"Has he admitted to doing all the things he did?" Emily asked.

The detective shook his head. "He's denying everything."

Emily frowned. "But he had the bat and the panties."

The detective nodded. "It was pretty damning evidence. I'm sure we have the right guy."

Emily gave him a shaky smile. "Thank you, Detective."

After the detective left, Emily sank into Cage's arms. "They caught him."

He nodded and stroked his hand over her hair. "Now, you can get back to a normal life."

She shook her head. "I can't move back into my apartment."

He smiled. "I'm sure Gunny would let you stay at the lodge indefinitely. He loves you like a daughter."

She leaned back and looked up into Cage's eyes. "What about us?" she asked.

"We won't need to stay up in the cabin anymore."

She pouted. "And here I was getting used to cold showers."

He laughed. "The case might be over, but I am hoping we aren't."

Emily leaned up on her toes and brushed her lips across his. "I feel the same."

"Good," Cage drew in a deep breath and let it out. "What's your schedule for the afternoon?"

"I only had one appointment, and he cancelled."

"Good, then let's get back out to the lodge and let

the folks know what's going on." He walked with her back to her office, where she gathered her purse and then he held the door for her. "The timing couldn't be better. Hank's supposed to be coming in tomorrow, and the celebration is on Friday."

Emily nodded. "I know. I took off the rest of the weekend just so I could help out."

"Then we'll have good cause to celebrate." He hugged her tightly then kissed her hard. They drove out of Colorado Springs, headed for the ranch.

Emily was hopeful for a bright future, now that she could get to know Cage better without the threat of a stalker hanging over them.

CHAPTER 16

THOUGH HE MISSED the solitude and intimacy of the miner's cabin, Cage was glad to sleep in a real bed in the lodge again.

After the police took Jimmy Rhodes away, he and Emily returned to Lost Valley and celebrated the capture of Emily's stalker by grilling steaks and drinking beer late into the evening.

Gunny, RJ and Jake had to cut out early to man Gunny's Watering Hole for the regulars, who expected it to be open and ready to serve them drinks and food.

They urged Cage and Emily to relax, reassuring them that the crowd would be small and their help wouldn't be needed.

The night got better when he and Emily retired to his bedroom where they made love into the wee hours of the morning and slept in.

After a late breakfast, Cage helped Gunny, Jake and Max set up a stage for the band that would be playing the next day for the grand opening of the Brotherhood Protectors Colorado Division.

RJ, JoJo and Emily strung twinkle lights and banners from the porch eaves. They helped Swede wire the stage for when the band arrived.

Hank, Kujo and their families didn't arrive until late that night, their flight plans having been delayed by weather.

Swede and Jake took two vehicles to the Colorado Springs Regional Airport to collect them. When they finally made it to the lodge, it was all hands on deck to get them moved into their rooms and settled for the night.

Hank had been informed of the capture of Emily's stalker the day before, and everything was set for the grand opening the following day.

Friday morning was a team effort to get the last-minute preparations complete for the guests who would be arriving at noon.

The band showed up a little before ten o'clock and set up their equipment on the stage. By eleven, they were warming up with a few easy listening country songs.

Sadie and Molly, Kujo's wife, did what they could to help in between corralling the little ones.

Kujo's retired Military Working Dog, Six, stayed at his master's side throughout the day.

The few times Emily disappeared out of his sight, Cage grew anxious. After being with her twenty-four-seven, he couldn't help worrying. Yes, they'd captured the stalker, but habits were hard to break. Especially when the habit was to be around Emily all the time.

Every time Emily came back in view, her smile lit Cage's day.

They hadn't really talked about what would happen next between them. It was as if they were avoiding the subject. Cage figured things might slow down a little bit between them to give them time to know each other better. Although, nothing had slowed down in the bedroom.

Even though the case had been resolved, Cage didn't want Emily to fade out of his life. He liked her a lot. In fact, he'd go so far as to say he loved her. But he didn't want to speak too soon for fear of jinxing their relationship.

The first limousines arrived at five minutes to twelve. Chauffeurs parked them in the grass where Max directed them and got out to open the doors for the occupants. One by one, well-dressed men and women gathered in the yard and on the porch.

Hank and Sadie greeted each personally and introduced the other members of the Brotherhood Protectors team.

Though she was a mega-movie star, Sadie wore blue jeans, cowboy boots and a white blouse. Her golden blond hair hung loose around her shoulders, and she smiled happily as she stood beside Hank, chatting with her friends.

"She could wear a potato sack and make it look good."

Cage turned to find Emily standing beside him, her gaze on Sadie and Hank.

"I prefer redheads," he said and pulled her into his arms for a quick kiss. "I didn't know it until I met you."

She laughed and leaned against him, smiling. "It's good to see Gunny, RJ and JoJo so happy. They deserve to be."

"As do you," Cage said.

She sighed. "I'm glad it's over. I hated looking over my shoulder every second of the day, not knowing when he would strike next or what he would do."

"Same." Cage turned her to face him. "But I'm not ready for us to be over."

She blew out a stream of air. "Whew. I'm glad you said that. I was beginning to wonder where you stood on the subject."

He laughed. "And I was wondering where you stood. Are we a go for a long-term relationship?"

Emily nodded. "I am, if you are."

He held her close and whispered in her ear. "I'd ask you to marry me right now, if I thought we were ready."

"I'd say yes, if I thought we were ready." She leaned back, her eyes shining. "Are you asking?"

"Are you ready?" he shot back.

She nodded.

"Then I'm asking," he said, his heart bursting.

Her smile spread across her face. "And I'm saying yes."

Cage kissed her, loving her more every second. When he finally raised his head, he rested his forehead on hers. "Should we tell everyone?"

Emily shook her head. "Not yet. Let them wonder why we have our heads together kissing so much."

Cage caught Jake and RJ looking their way, grins on their faces. "Yeah, well, it won't take long for them to guess. Not when we're grinning like we won the lottery."

More cars and trucks arrived, parking on the grass in a nearby field. Locals mingled with the celebrities, and the band played. Food was laid out on long tables, banquet style, but Hank and Sadie wanted to make the official announcement before eating could commence.

Jake asked the band to stop playing and handed a microphone to Hank.

"Thank you for coming to the Lost Valley Ranch, the new headquarters for the Brotherhood Protectors Colorado Division. From the start, the Brotherhood Protectors' mission has been to provide security services to whomever might need them.

We've helped many people in Montana and have now expanded our operations to Colorado. We hire the best of the best, former military heroes you can trust with your lives. They've proven themselves on the battlefield and are now proving themselves here on our home front."

Hank waved a hand toward Jake. "I'd like to thank Jake Cogburn for leading the effort to establish the team here in Colorado. He's done a fine job hiring staff and is now ready to put them to work."

Jake gave Hank a chin lift.

Hank waved toward Gunny. "I'd also like to thank Dan Tate, the owner of Lost Valley Ranch, for giving us a place to call home in Colorado."

Gunny raised a hand and nodded in acknowledgement. "Call me Gunny."

Hank continued. "And most of all, I'd like to thank my beautiful wife, Sadie, for believing in my vision and supporting my decision to start and expand this great organization." He grinned. "Thank you all for coming to the grand opening of the Brotherhood Protectors Colorado. Now, don't let me keep you from the food Gunny and his staff have prepared."

The band resumed playing and the crowd surged toward the buffet table to fill their plates.

"I'll be right back," Emily said.

"Where are you going?"

"I forgot to put serving spoons in the baked beans and potato salad."

"I'll come with you." Cage said and started to follow her.

Before Cage could catch up with Emily, Hank approached him with a sharply dressed woman, wearing a long, cream-colored dress and a broad-brimmed hat like the ones women wore to the derby.

Hank turned to the woman and smiled as he introduced her. "Cage, I'd like to introduce Lauren Mathis, Sadie's costar in the movie that will come out next month. Lauren lives on a ranch here in Colorado. She wanted to meet all of the men currently employed with the Colorado division. Lauren, this is Cage Weaver."

The woman removed her sunglasses and held out her hand.

Cage really wanted to follow Emily to the kitchen, but he didn't want to appear rude in front of a potential customer. He took her hand and nodded. "Nice to meet you, Ms. Mathis."

Her lips were painted with a shiny red lipstick, and when she smiled, the woman was beautiful.

But she wasn't Emily.

"What branch of the service were you in?" she asked.

"Army."

Hank added, "Cage was an Army Ranger."

Lauren's smile widened. "My father was an Army Ranger. He was a good man. I have a fondness for men who've served in the military, especially those who were Rangers. Thank you for your service."

"Thank you for your support," Cage said.

"I'm certain I will have need of your team's services. I know the value of your training and respect your dedication to our country."

She wasn't what he'd expected. Behind the fancy clothes was a woman who cared. Cage gave her a genuine smile. "Thank you, ma'am. Now, if you'll excuse me, I need to help out in the kitchen."

She grinned. "Please, don't let me keep you."

"Hank, hang on a minute," Jake called out. "You, too, Cage. I want you to meet someone."

Cage glanced toward a truck that had just parked. Two men climbed out and headed their direction. They had short, tight haircuts and carried themselves with a military bearing that was easily recognized.

Jake hurried toward them, shook their hands, and then led them to where Hank, Cage and Lauren stood. "Hank, Cage and Miss Mathis, this is former Navy SEAL Sawyer Johnson and former 10th Special Forces operative Lorenzo Ramos, the two newest members of our team."

Cage shook their hands. "Nice to meet you both." While he really wanted to get away to help Emily, he couldn't leave without being rude.

Lorenzo nodded. "Call me Enzo. Only my mother calls me Lorenzo, and only when I'm in trouble."

Cage nodded. "Enzo, nice to meet you."

Sawyer glanced past Cage and frowned. "Is there supposed to be smoke coming from that barn?"

Cage, Jake and Hank spun on their heels.

A column of dark smoke rose from the back side of the barn.

"Gunny!" Cage called out.

Gunny was already running toward the barn, followed by Max, RJ and JoJo.

Hank and Jake raced after them.

Cage split off and headed for the lodge, a bad feeling in his gut. He wanted to know Emily was safe before he tackled a fire.

EMILY HAD BEEN FISHING SERVING spoons out of a drawer when she heard someone yell for help from the back porch. She dropped what she'd been holding and ran to see what was wrong.

She ran out on the porch and looked around but didn't see anyone. She frowned. "Who's there?"

"Me," a voice said behind her.

She turned and was hit by an electrical charge that shot fire through her body and made her muscles completely collapse.

Her body was paralyzed and her mind confused and disoriented.

A man leaned over her and smiled. "I will have you," he whispered.

She knew that face. She struggled to put a name to it in her befuddled state.

Nathan Small. His name was Nathan Small.

But his names didn't start with a J or an R. Then a memory struck her from her first meeting with the man. He'd complained that his records were always getting mixed with his father's since they had the same name. He wasn't just Nathan Small. He was Nathan Small, Jr.

The letters JR weren't initials, they stood for junior.

Now that she knew, she couldn't do anything about it. She couldn't call out, couldn't move.

Nathan grabbed her arm and slung her over his shoulder in a fireman's hold and carried her out to a two-seater ATV. He dumped her in the passenger side and strapped her in. Then he started the engine, the sound likely masked by the music from the band on the other side of the lodge.

No one would hear the sound. No one would know he'd taken her.

"Your friends won't think to look for you for a little while. They'll be too worried about the fire I started in a pile of straw behind the barn."

He drove through an open gate, out into a field away from the lodge and onto a trail that led to a high mountain meadow where the cattle liked to graze in the summer.

With little control of her body, Emily bounced and jolted with each bump they rolled over. Where was he taking her and why? They weren't heading back to the road; they were going higher into the mountains. If he planned to get away with her, he wasn't heading the right direction.

Unless he wasn't planning to get away with her.

The longer he drove, the farther away they got from the people who could help her.

Knowing she'd been tased, she knew her muscles could take up to fifteen minutes to fully recover. If she wanted to get away from Nathan, she had to regain control of her own body first.

She willed strength into her fingers and toes. Little by little, she could move them and then her arms and legs. But not enough to fight off a man who weighed at least a hundred pounds more than her.

When he finally pulled to a stop, she was blinded by the glare of sunshine off the surface of the clear mountain lake she used to picnic beside with RJ and JoJo.

"Here's where the trail ends." Nathan climbed out of the ATV and came around to unbuckle her seatbelt.

It hadn't been a full fifteen minutes, but enough time had elapsed that Emily had control of her muscles. But she didn't want him to know it until she was in a position to get away.

Once again, he grabbed one of her arms, dragged her out of the ATV and bent to throw her over his shoulder again. When he lowered his head, she raised her knee sharply, aiming for his nose.

She heard a sharp crack.

Nathan yelled, staggered backward and clutched a hand to his nose as blood ran down his face.

Emily scrambled to her feet and ran. Her legs were wobbly. She tried but couldn't move fast enough to get away before Nathan hit her again with the stun gun.

This time, he held it against her. Pain shot through her, and she fell to the ground.

"Why did you have to go and do that?" he said. "I only want to be with you. And I will have you, despite the fact you've been sleeping with another man."

He didn't lift her and carry her this time. Instead, he grabbed both of her wrists and dragged her across the gravel toward the lake.

Her head spun, and her thoughts were scrambled. What was he doing? Why was he dragging her toward the water?

"You're the only woman who ever listened to me. I know you love me, not that other guy. He'll never love you like I do. Never."

He slowed and came to a stop on the shore. "Don't you see? You belong to me. You and I were meant to be together. I gave you roses. I gave you my heart."

He pulled something from his pocket and held it over her head. "I carried a part of you with me."

It was a pair of her lace panties he'd stolen from her apartment.

"Now, we will always be together. You and me forever. No one will find us and keep us apart."

He left her on the shore, went back to the ATV and drove it to the edge of the trail, climbed out and gave it a hard shove.

The vehicle disappeared down a steep incline, making a loud crashing noise down below.

Emily's head stopped spinning as the effects of the stun gun waned. She still couldn't move her muscles enough to run.

Nathan returned, took her wrists in his hands and walked into the lake, pulling her along with him.

The icy water wrapped around her, dragging at her clothes, sucking her downward.

Nathan didn't stop until he stood in water up to his chest. He pulled her into his arms and held her close. "The cold quits hurting when your body goes numb," he whispered, his teeth chattering. "It won't be long, and I'll have you to myself forever."

Nathan moved deeper, until the water was up to his neck.

Emily floated along with him, unable to move from the effects of the stun gun and, now, the freezing cold numbing her limbs.

Was this how it would end? Would she drown with a deranged man, never to see Cage again?

Nathan moved another step, taking her under with him.

CHAPTER 17

CAGE ARRIVED in the kitchen to find it empty. He looked in the pantry and still couldn't find her. Knowing Emily, if she had glanced out the back door and seen the smoke coming up behind the barn, she would have gone out to help.

Cage burst through the back door about the time the band stopped playing.

The sound of a small engine caught his attention, and he looked out across the yard to where a gate stood open. He caught a glimpse of a two-seater ATV heading across a pasture into the tree line. His gut told him Emily was in that ATV, and she hadn't gotten in of her own free will.

His heart in his throat, Cage raced for the barn, threw open the door and ran inside to where the four-wheelers were parked in the far corner. Smoke drifted through the cracks in the wood, but the fire wasn't inside the barn, but behind it.

He jumped on one of the four-wheelers, started the engine and raced toward the door.

RJ appeared in front of him.

He swerved to miss her and nearly ran into a wall.

"What are you doing?" she asked.

"It's Emily." Cage struggled to point the ATV toward the door. "Someone's taken her."

"Where?" RJ called out.

"Through the gate behind the lodge," he said.

"That doesn't lead to a road. All the trails leading out of that pasture go up to a lake."

"Then there's no time to lose. We have to get to her."

RJ ran for the back at the barn and jumped on one of the four wheelers. "Wait for me. I know the shortest route."

"Catch up with me. I'm not waiting." Cage hit the throttle and raced out of the barn.

Jake waved at him as he went by. "Where are you going?"

"Emily," he called out and leaned forward on the ATV, aiming for the back of the lodge and the open gate leading into the pasture.

RJ caught up, passed him and led the way into the trees where a trail wound up the side of the mountain.

As they neared the top, movement caught Cage's eye.

The ATV he'd seen leaving the back of the lodge pitched over the ridge ahead.

RJ had to dodge the vehicle as it crashed down the side of the hill into the trees.

Cage's heart leaped in his chest until he realized the seats had been empty. He gunned the throttle and flew up the reminder of the trail, shooting over the top to a flat area where a lake spread before him.

Something dark bobbed in the water, and then sank below the surface.

Cage didn't hesitate, he drove straight for the lake. When he reached the edge of the lake, he dove off the ATV and into the water. The cold hit him like a bolt of electricity, shocking his body with its intensity.

He powered past the pain and swam out to where he'd last seen something on the surface. Sucking in a deep breath, he dove down, reaching ahead of him with his hand. When he touched something, he grabbed it and pulled it to the surface with him.

As he came up, a strong arm wrapped around his leg and yanked him under.

He kicked and fought his way free. But his other leg was captured, and he was dragged down again.

This time when Cage surfaced, he gulped air and dove down, fighting off the man who was keeping him from getting to Emily.

He gripped the man's arm, pulled him up,

wrapped his arm around his neck and snapped his head to one side.

The man went limp.

Cage shoved him to the side, gulped more air and dove to the bottom of the lake. The silt at the bottom was stirred up, making it too murky to see clearly. He had to feel his way along the bottom, praying he would find Emily before it was too late.

When his fingers tangled in hair, he grabbed a handful and shot for the surface. Once there, he floated her onto her back.

It was Emily, and she wasn't breathing.

Cage knew he had to get her out of the cold water before she succumbed to hypothermia. As it was, his limbs were numbing and not working at full potential. He swam for the shore.

RJ had waded in up to her hips. She grabbed Emily under her arms and dragged her through the water. When they reached the shore, Cage lifted her legs. They laid her out on dry land and rolled her onto her stomach.

Cage straddled her hips and pushed the water out of her lungs.

"She's still not breathing on her own," RJ said.

Cage flipped her onto her back, pinched her nose and breathed into her mouth. He did it again and again.

RJ felt Emily's neck. "I have pulse. Weak, but there."

Suddenly, Emily coughed and spit out water.

Cage sat her up and pulled her into his arms. But he was as wet as she was and couldn't give her the warmth she needed.

Two four-wheelers and one two-seater shot over the top of the trail and came to a stop a few feet away.

Jake and Max leaped off their ATVs, stripping out of their shirts.

Gunny came up behind them, handing over his shirt and the T-shirt he'd had on beneath it. "We need to get her back to the lodge and bring her body temperature back up ASAP."

His body shaking from the cold, Cage lifted Emily from the ground and carried her to the two-seater.

"You can't hold her all the way," Jake said. "You're too cold."

Cage didn't want to let go of Emily, but Jake was right.

Jake sat in the passenger seat. Cage laid Emily in his lap and Gunny slid in behind the steering wheel.

Emily reached for Cage. "You found me."

"Damn right, I did," he said. "I'll see you at the lodge." He looked to Gunny. "Go."

Cage mounted his four-wheeler and followed Emily all the way to the bottom of the trail. Then he sped ahead of the two-seater, arriving at the lodge before they did.

He had JoJo running for blankets and heating pads and Sadie drawing a bathtub full of warm water.

When Emily was brought into the lodge, Jake carried her straight up the stairs to the bathroom where he settled her into the bathtub, clothes and all.

Cage knelt on the floor beside her, shivering and holding her hand.

Emily smiled up at him, her teeth chattering. "You're cold, too."

He nodded.

RJ wrapped a towel around his shoulders. "The sheriff is on his way to deal with the body. I'll leave you two alone." She exited the bathroom and closed the door behind her.

"Get in," Emily slid to the side as much as she could.

"No," he said. "Not until your body temperature is back to normal."

"What about yours?"

"I'll be fine. I wasn't the one who almost drowned."

She leaned her head back and closed her eyes. "He hit me with a stun gun. I couldn't move a single muscle to save myself."

"That bastard." He felt no remorse for snapping the man's neck.

She opened her eyes and reached for his hand. "All I thought about was the fact I wouldn't get to see you again."

He chuckled though he felt more like crying. "You scared ten years off my life."

"We had it wrong," she said.

"What did we have wrong?" he said, holding her hand beneath the warm water.

"Nathan Small was a junior."

Cage frowned. "That was his name?"

Emily nodded. "Nathan Small, Jr."

"JR was for junior?" Cage squeezed her hand. "He set up Jimmy with the bat and panties."

Emily nodded.

"That doesn't excuse what Jimmy did to you," Cage said.

"No, but he wasn't the stalker. Nathan was."

"And he will never threaten you again."

Emily frowned. "He won't."

Cage met her gaze. "Never."

Emily sighed. "I should feel bad, but I don't. I believe I'll need to schedule an appointment for myself to work through PTSD for almost drowning." She shook her head. "I never want to go through that again. Even this tub full of water is giving me the heebie-jeebies."

"I promise not to let you drown, but you have to stay until you're warm."

"I'm warm," she said. "And I'm ready to snuggle in bed with lots of blankets and you."

He grinned. "That can be arranged."

Cage helped her out of the water, stripped her

wet clothes off and dried her off with a couple of big fluffy towels. Then he carried her into his room, wrapped her in a dozen blankets and laid her in the bed.

"I'll be back in a flash." He left her long enough to duck into the bathroom to get a hot shower and dry off. Two minutes later, he was back across the hall, wearing a towel and a smile.

RJ caught him going into his room. "Is Emily warmer?"

"She is, and about to get even warmer." He winked, stepped into the room and closed the door behind him.

He settled in the blankets, wrapping his arms around her. "For the record, I love you."

"For the record," she said, "ditto."

EPILOGUE

CAGE STOOD with the box holding Ryan's ashes at the edge of the summit of Pikes Peak.

The sun shone down on them from a bright, beautiful Colorado sky. At 14,111 feet, the air was cool, the wind brisk and the view seemingly endless.

"Well, Ryan, you'd be happy to know, I'm well on my way to fulfilling our dreams. I finished the Pikes Peak Marathon, I found the woman I want to spend the rest of my life with, and someday soon, I hope to have a couple of kids with her. If we have a son, we've agreed to name him after a military hero. I voted for Patton."

"Don't listen to him, Ryan," Emily said as she stood beside Cage, the wind whipping her auburn curls around her cheeks.

"Just kidding, buddy," Cage said. "His name will be Ryan, after the best friend a guy could have ever had. I miss you, but it helps to know you're finally going to learn to fly." He glanced toward Emily. "Are we all clear?"

Emily looked back toward the visitors' center. "There are half a dozen tourists taking pictures in front of the sign. None of them are looking this way. Now would be a good time...if you're ready."

Cage knelt on the ground, opened the box and let the wind do the rest.

Emily knelt beside him and wrapped her arm around his waist. "I would have liked Ryan," she said.

"He would have loved you." Tears slid down Cage's face as he said a silent goodbye to his friend. His brother. His family.

He rose to his feet, helped Emily to hers and stuffed the empty box into his backpack. They stood for a long moment, watching the ashes lift and float away in the wind.

Then Cage turned Emily in his arms. "Ready?"

She nodded, leaned up on her toes and kissed his lips. "I'm ready for whatever the future will hold for us."

He nodded, his heart swelling with the love he felt for this woman. "As long as we're together."

TACTICAL TAKEOVER

BROTHERHOOD PROTECTORS
COLORADO BOOK #4

New York Times & USA Today
Bestselling Author

ELLE JAMES

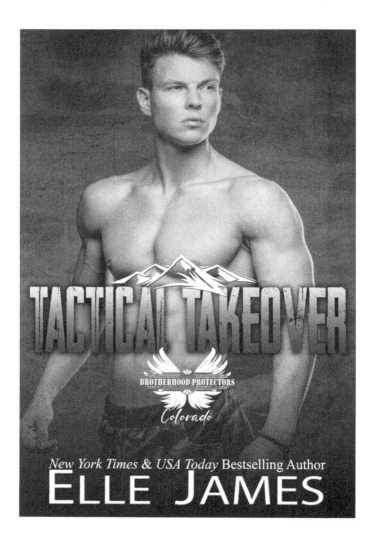

TACTICAL TAKEOVER

BROTHERHOOD PROTECTORS

Colorado

New York Times & USA Today Bestselling Author

ELLE JAMES

CHAPTER 1

Sawyer Johnson folded his long, lean form into the airplane seat, his knees touching the back of the seat in front of him.

Rain splattered the window beside him, the clouds in Denver seeming to sit on the airport.

Passengers filed slowly past his row on their way to assigned seats. As one man stopped to attempt to shove an oversized suitcase into the overhead bin, everyone came to a standstill.

After a two-hour weather delay, the crew was eager to get the plane in the air and on its way to their final stop...Colorado Springs.

After three attempts to fit a fat suitcase into a narrow slot, the passenger pulled it free and forced everyone standing in the aisles to back up to the exit door in order to have the bag tagged and stored in the belly of the aircraft.

Once again, the line of people moved past him, filling the seats, with the flight attendant urging them to sit and stow their belongings beneath the seat in front of them. She added that the sooner they all were seated, the sooner boarding would be completed, and they'd be on their way.

After the aisles cleared, Sawyer eyed the empty seat beside him, hoping it would remain empty so that he could move over and let his left leg stretch out into the aisle. Rehab had returned most of its functionality, but long bouts of sitting with his leg bent caused his leg to stiffen.

The flight attendant moved from the rear to the front of the aircraft, counting souls. When she arrived at the front, she nodded toward the ground crew indicating they could close the hatch.

A shout sounded from the jet bridge. "Wait!"

The attendant stepped backward to let a woman with sandy-blond hair race on board.

As soon as the blonde was through the door, she slowed her pace, ran a hand over her hair and walked down the aisle with her chin up, daring anyone to say anything about her entrance.

The hatch closed, the attendant checked the lock and lifted the phone. "Ladies and gentlemen, welcome aboard. As soon as we're all seated, we'll be on our way."

The woman checked the numbers above the seats and finally stopped beside Sawyer's row. She struggled to fit her small suitcase into the overhead bin, and then started to slide into the space beside him. Before she sat, she stopped. "If you want the aisle, I don't mind switching." She spoke in a soft southern accent that reminded him of a basket of deep-fried chicken and sweat-soaked glasses of iced tea.

"Are you sure?" he asked, pulling the latch up on the belt to release it.

"Positive." She smiled tightly. "I don't like flying, but it helps if I can see out the window as we take off and land."

Using his good arm, he pushed to his feet and stepped past her into the aisle.

The woman slid into the seat against the window, and Sawyer dropped into the seat beside her.

He had to loosen the seatbelt all the way in order to chase the other side of the buckle one-handed.

A flight attendant walked by at that time, reached down, connected the two ends of the buckle and smiled. She didn't say a word, just moved down the aisles closing overhead bins.

Heat burned up Sawyer's neck and into his cheeks. He didn't like it when people helped him. He had to figure out things for himself, including buckling his own seatbelt using his good hand.

"I feel bad that I'm the last person on the plane," the woman beside him murmured. "I hope I didn't hold us up too much."

"It's been a difficult day in the airports," Sawyer

commiserated. "I almost didn't get off the ground in Dallas because of the storms here in the Denver area."

"Exactly," the young woman said. "My flight from Atlanta was over two hours late and barely made it here in time for me to make this flight. I was supposed to have a long layover before I boarded the flight for Colorado Springs. And then the pilot almost had to divert to another airport because of the weather over Denver. We went around twice before the ceiling lifted enough for us to land." She raised the window screen and stared out at the runway. "I hope it's clear enough for us to get off the ground."

"It should be. Going out is easier than coming in under limited visibility conditions," Sawyer explained.

Still staring out the window at the rain-soaked airport, the woman sighed. "I just need to get to Colorado Springs. The sooner the better." She turned to face him. "I'm sorry." She gave him a crooked grin. "You don't need to hear me complain."

"It's okay. You're only echoing my thoughts. I'm ready to be in Colorado Springs myself."

She cocked an eyebrow. "Business or pleasure?"

He lifted a shoulder and let it drop. "Both, I guess. The pleasure part of it is up for debate. I'm going to check out a potential job offer and subsequent move to the area. What about you?"

Her smile turned upside down. "I gave up a good

job in Savannah, Georgia, to come out here. I hope I don't regret it."

Sawyer studied the woman. "You don't sound pleased to be moving out here."

"I kind of had to. My brother landed out here at one of the ski resorts. He's been living here since late last fall."

Sawyer tipped his head toward the rainy window. "Not much skiing going on during the summer season."

She snorted. "True. And he's had entirely too much time on his hands."

He glanced her way. "Getting into trouble?"

She nodded, opened her mouth to say something and closed it when the plane rolled backward. Her hand came up to grip his, and her eyes widened.

Even though the woman's grip on his good hand was tight, Sawyer didn't try to disengage.

As the plane taxied out to the runway, his seat mate must have realized she was holding his hand, because she let go and grimaced. "I'm sorry. The landing coming into Denver shook me. I admit I'm not looking forward to this short stretch to Colorado Springs."

She clutched her hands together in her lap and laughed nervously. "I don't usually hold hands with strangers."

Sawyer was just glad she'd held on tight. He was glad. He could help allay her fears. "No worries." He held out his right hand. "Since we're already past the awkward stage of touching a stranger's hand, I'm Sawyer Johnson."

She took his hand. "Kinsley Brothers," she said. "And thank you for not being offended."

"How could I be offended by a nice-looking young woman holding my hand?" After a brief shake, he let go and returned his hand to his lap.

That brief exchange had sent little bursts of electricity running up his arm and into his chest. He'd never felt anything like it and wondered if it was a residual effect of having had half his body blown up by an improvised explosive device.

Since the electrical impulses had happened to his uninjured side, he wasn't sure it had anything to do with the damage done that had ended the life of his buddy and Sawyer's career as a Navy SEAL. She was pretty hot and totally desirable.

Too bad he wasn't in any shape to ask her out. Though he'd regained much of his physical strength, he had yet to recover mentally. Thus, his reluctance in accepting the job offer from Hank Patterson, the founder of Brotherhood Protectors.

"Thanks," Kinsley said. "I appreciate that you didn't take it the wrong way." Her eyes widened. "Oh, dear Lord. I'm not going to get you in trouble for that, am I? I mean, you're not married, are you?"

Sawyer snorted. "Been there, almost did that. Didn't work out. So, no, I'm not married."

"Whew." She brushed a hand across her forehead. "Well, for me anyway."

"And for me," he assured her.

Kinsley shook her head. "Wow, I'm opening my mouth and inserting both feet, aren't I?" She looked out the window as they lined up on the runway. "I tend to rattle on when I'm nervous or scared."

"It's okay to be nervous or scared when flying. I was always a little tense on takeoffs and landings. It got better with repetition, but I never completely got over it." He gave her a weak smile. "And I've been up hundreds of times."

"And it doesn't get better?" She glanced his way as she chewed on her bottom lip.

"Not really. I just learned to compensate…think about something else."

She laughed without humor. "Unfortunately, everything I have to think about at the moment has me nervous or scared."

"Moving to another state, starting a new job…I get it. Change can be unnerving."

Her hands twisted in her lap. "And I'm doing it to be closer to my brother. I'm afraid he's into something he shouldn't be."

"How so?"

The plane's jet engines revved, and the pilot let off the brakes. Starting slowly, at first, the aircraft rolled down the runway, picking up speed quickly. Rain pounded against the wings and windows.

Kinsley reached for the armrest, encountered his hand and gripped his fingers so tightly, Sawyer worried she'd cut off the circulation.

The nose of the plane tilted upward. In the next second, the craft left the ground and rose into the air.

When they encountered the sky's ceiling, the plane bounced and jolted as if the clouds they'd entered weren't fluffy puffs of spun sugar but more like hard speed bumps.

Sawyer wasn't sure how she did it, but Kinsley's grip tightened.

While gaining altitude, the plane tipped to the right, away from the mountains, making a wide turn to head south toward their destination.

They hadn't completely finished the turn when the plane encountered a wind shear and plunged a couple hundred feet in less than a second.

Women screamed, and men cursed. Loose items were slung around the interior of the cabin.

Kinsley let go of Sawyer's hand and hooked her arm through his, burying her face against his shoulder. "We're gonna die."

"No...we're not." Sawyer clamped her arm beneath his and let her burrow her face into his shoulder. "We're going to Colorado Springs, and we'll arrive safely."

The captain's voice came over the loudspeaker. "I'm sorry folks. We just got word from the Colorado Springs airport. They're getting hammered by a hailstorm right now, and the wind is pushing another front through in the next thirty minutes. We're circling Denver International Airport to land. The agents at the gate will work with you to get you onto the first flight out in the morning."

A collective groan sounded from the passengers.

Kinsley chewed on her bottom lip, her eyebrows forming a V in the middle of her forehead. "I need to get there as soon as possible."

Sawyer stared out the window at the heavy clouds. "You do realize it's only an hour and a half drive, don't you?"

She glanced his way. "Is that all?"

He nodded. "Look, I don't want to spend a night in Denver any more than you do. If there are any available, I'm going to rent a car and drive down tonight. You can ride with me if you like."

"For that matter," her eyes narrowed, "I could rent one myself."

"You could," he agreed. "If you were planning to rent a car when you arrived in Colorado Springs, you might as well do it here in Denver."

"Is that what you were going to do... rent a car in Colorado Springs?" she asked.

He shook his head. "Not actually. I had someone coming to pick me up at the airport to take me out to where I'll be staying temporarily."

"Then it doesn't make sense for you to rent the

car. I should, and you can ride with me. Unless you prefer to be in control." She cocked an eyebrow.

He held up his hands, grinning. "I don't need to be in control. But you should let me pay half."

"That won't be necessary," Kinsley said. "I will be keeping the rental for a while. I have it planned into my budget for this trip."

"I'd take you up on the offer, but I'm going further than Colorado Springs. I'm headed for Fool's Gold, on the other side of the mountains from the Springs."

"Wow, me too. I'm going first to Fool's Gold."

He frowned. "Why Fool's Gold?"

She nodded. "It'll be my jumping off point." She glanced at her watch. "I'll have to stay the night somewhere."

"Do you already have a room?"

She shook her head. "No. I figured I'd find one when I get there."

"I understand Fool's Gold is a small tourist town. I'm not sure how many hotels are out there. You might end up going back to Colorado Springs to find a decent place to stay the night."

"I'd really like to be in Fool's Gold tonight, if at all possible. I need to find my brother."

"You don't know where he is?"

As the plane landed, Kinsley turned off the airplane mode on her cellphone and brought up an image of a map with a blue dot in the center.

"I have an app on my phone that allows me to find

my brother's cellphone. The boy carries it with him everywhere." Her eyebrows descended. "At least, he used to carry it everywhere." She held up the map for him to see. "That blue dot is the last place the application found his phone." She drew in a shaky breath. "That was a week ago. I haven't heard from him since."

"Could he have lost his phone?"

She shrugged. "Maybe. But he would've found another way to contact me. He promised to check in with me every other day." She brought up her text messages and handed it to Sawyer. "This is the last message I got from my brother."

He glanced down at the words on the cellphone screen.

You know the group I told you about that I joined out here? I think I made a mistake. Only now that I'm in...I'm not quite sure how to get out.

Sawyer's hand tightened on the cellphone. "That doesn't sound good."

Her lips pressed into a thin line. "Tell me about it. That's why I'm on this plane, headed to the mountains. I don't know where exactly he is, but I have to find him."

"Where are your parents? Do they know what's

happening? I assume they're still alive and would like to know what's going on."

She gave him a slight smile. "They're on a world cruise and aren't expected to return for another two months. I'd hate to bring them back, and I'm not sure I know how."

"So, you're on your way to the mountains to bring your brother back on your own?" Sawyer shook his head. "What if he's mixed up with one of the anarchists' groups? You're not…" He waved a hand.

Her brow rose. "A man?"

"No. I could be wrong, but you're not trained for combat, are you?"

She chewed on her bottom lip. "No. I'm not."

"Even if you were, you can't go charging into one of their camps, demanding anything. They might shoot first, rather than ask questions."

Her mouth screwed into a twist. "Great. Now you've got me more scared than I was to begin with. I thought I'd drive out there, tell Derek to get into the car and get the hell out of Dodge."

"It all depends on who he's hooked up with." Sawyer shrugged. "It could go the way you said."

"Or not," she whispered. "I don't know what else to do."

The plane rolled to a stop at the gate, and people stood to collect their bags from the overhead bins.

Sawyer rose from his seat and, with his good

hand, pulled her suitcase out of the overhead bin and set it in the seat he'd vacated.

"Thank you," she said with a smile.

He retrieved his backpack out of the overhead bin, looped it over his shoulder then stepped back to allow her to emerge into the aisle.

"So, are you riding with me to Fool's Gold?" Kinsley asked.

"Do you trust me?"

She glanced up at him, her eyes narrowing. Then a smile spread across her face. "Actually, I do."

He figured a lot had to do with the fact he had one bum arm. What man could molest a woman if he had one useless limb? Sawyer sighed. "I'm glad. I'll even drive if you want me to. It's no fun to drive in the dark, much less the rain."

Kinsley lifted her chin. "I'll drive. But you have to stay awake to keep me awake. I'm already tired as I've been up since four-thirty this morning to get to the airport for my flight out of Savannah."

"Deal. I'll stay awake. But we might want to stop for coffee on the way."

She grinned. "We can do that. I could use the caffeine, too."

With the jet bridge in place, the door to the aircraft opened, and the flight attendant moved back to allow people to exit the aircraft.

"I guess we just have to hit baggage claim and the rental car counter," Sawyer said.

"I only brought my carry-on," Kinsley said. "What about you?"

He tipped his head toward the backpack over his shoulder. "I have everything."

"Good. There might be a rush for the rental car counter. I'd like to get there as quickly as possible," Kinsley said.

"Let's do this." Sawyer followed Kinsley off the airplane, working the kinks out of his stiff leg. Once it was in motion, he had no trouble with it. He'd even gotten back into running before he'd left Maryland.

Kinsley set her carry-on bag on its wheels and hurried alongside Sawyer, following the signs to the rental car counters.

Fortunately, they found a company without a line that had an SUV that fit Kinsley's needs, considering she might be traipsing around the backcountry to find her brother and would need something that could get into places a car couldn't access.

Within twenty minutes of exiting the aircraft, Sawyer found himself seated in the passenger seat beside someone who'd been a perfect stranger before they'd boarded the airplane in Denver.

"You sure you're okay with me hitching a ride with you? I mean, we only just met."

She nodded. "I am. Besides, while you weren't looking, I snapped a photo of you and sent it to a friend back home." She grinned. "If I don't contact her when I get to my hotel by midnight, she's to contact the Colorado State Police and file a missing and endangered person report."

Sawyer laughed. "Good for you. That puts the onus on me to make sure you find a room before midnight."

"Damn right, it does." Then she focused her attention on the road leading out of the airport in the driving rain.

"If you don't mind, I'm going to call ahead to let my contacts know I won't be flying into Colorado Springs. That way they won't head all the way into the airport."

"Go for it. At least you have someone expecting you in Fool's Gold." Her pretty lips twisted. "Must be nice."

He hated that she was on her own for the task she'd taken on.

Pulling his cellphone out of his pocket, he dialed Jake Cogburn's number. He was the man Hank had connected him with for the job in Colorado. Hank led the team in Montana. Jake, or Cog, as Hank had referred to the man, was the lead over the Colorado division of the Brotherhood Protectors. He'd be Sawyer's boss.

Jake answered on the first ring. "Sawyer, I heard that your flight was canceled."

"Hopefully, you saw that before anyone headed for the airport in the Springs," Sawyer said.

"I'd only made it to Fool's Gold before RJ called

and let me know. I turned around and came back to the ranch. I figured you'd be calling with an update."

"That's right," Sawyer said. "Rather than wait for morning, I'll be driving in. Should be there in around two hours."

"Great. I'll be up to show you where you'll be staying."

"Thanks."

"See you soon. Be careful out there. This storm isn't supposed to let up for a while."

With his boss notified, Sawyer ended the call and focused his attention on the woman driving. She was feisty and had a good head on her shoulders. He liked a strong woman who was loyal to her family.

There had to be a way to help her find her brother.

ABOUT THE AUTHOR

ELLE JAMES also writing as MYLA JACKSON is a *New York Times* and *USA Today* Bestselling author of books including cowboys, intrigues and paranormal adventures that keep her readers on the edges of their seats. When she's not at her computer, she's traveling, snow skiing, boating, or riding her ATV, dreaming up new stories. Learn more about Elle James at www.ellejames.com

Website | Facebook | Twitter | GoodReads | Newsletter | BookBub | Amazon

Or visit her alter ego Myla Jackson at mylajackson.com
Website | Facebook | Twitter | Newsletter

Follow Me!
www.ellejames.com
ellejames@ellejames.com

ALSO BY ELLE JAMES

Three Courageous Words

Four Relentless Days

Five Ways to Surrender

Six Minutes to Midnight

Hearts & Heroes Series

Wyatt's War (#1)

Mack's Witness (#2)

Ronin's Return (#3)

Sam's Surrender (#4)

Take No Prisoners Series

SEAL's Honor (#1)

SEAL'S Desire (#2)

SEAL's Embrace (#3)

SEAL's Obsession (#4)

SEAL's Proposal (#5)

SEAL's Seduction (#6)

SEAL'S Defiance (#7)

SEAL's Deception (#8)

SEAL's Deliverance (#9)

SEAL's Ultimate Challenge (#10)

Texas Billionaire Club

Tarzan & Janine (#1)

Cajun Magic Mysteries Books 1-3

SEAL Of My Own
Navy SEAL Survival

Navy SEAL Captive

Navy SEAL To Die For

Navy SEAL Six Pack

Devil's Shroud Series
Deadly Reckoning (#1)

Deadly Engagement (#2)

Deadly Liaisons (#3)

Deadly Allure (#4)

Deadly Obsession (#5)

Deadly Fall (#6)

Covert Cowboys Inc Series
Triggered (#1)

Taking Aim (#2)

Bodyguard Under Fire (#3)

Cowboy Resurrected (#4)

Navy SEAL Justice (#5)

Navy SEAL Newlywed (#6)

High Country Hideout (#7)

Clandestine Christmas (#8)

Thunder Horse Series

Hostage to Thunder Horse (#1)

Thunder Horse Heritage (#2)

Thunder Horse Redemption (#3)

Christmas at Thunder Horse Ranch (#4)

Demon Series

Hot Demon Nights (#1)

Demon's Embrace (#2)

Tempting the Demon (#3)

Lords of the Underworld

Witch's Initiation (#1)

Witch's Seduction (#2)

The Witch's Desire (#3)

Possessing the Witch (#4)

Stealth Operations Specialists (SOS)

Nick of Time

Alaskan Fantasy

Boys Behaving Badly Anthologies

Rogues (#1)

Blue Collar (#2)

Pirates (#3)

Stranded (#4)

First Responder (#5)

Blown Away

Warrior's Conquest

Enslaved by the Viking Short Story

Conquests

Smokin' Hot Firemen

Protecting the Colton Bride

Protecting the Colton Bride & Colton's Cowboy Code

Heir to Murder

Secret Service Rescue

High Octane Heroes

Haunted

Engaged with the Boss

Cowboy Brigade

Time Raiders: The Whisper

Bundle of Trouble

Killer Body

Operation XOXO

An Unexpected Clue

Baby Bling

Under Suspicion, With Child

Texas-Size Secrets

Cowboy Sanctuary

Lakota Baby

Dakota Meltdown

Beneath the Texas Moon

Made in the USA
Monee, IL
11 November 2023

46287135R00157